COME IN, I

By the Same Author

Georges Vandine: a novel revised edition 2011

Your Skyward eyes: a poetry collection, 33 bird poems and others 2011

Openings and Endgame: a collection of 14 short stories 2013

My name is Max: a novel with 23 photographs by Chris Redgrave 2014

Four Exits to Smolensk: a novel revised edition 2015

Bernard Parkes: a novel revised edition 2015

The Finder of Faces: a collection of 25 short stories revised edition 2016

Lavretsky: a novel revised edition 2016

Austin to Mons: a novel revised edition 2018

Asser of Sherborne: a historical novel revised edition 2019

James and Thomas Cranmer: a novel revised edition 2020

This way, I cried: a second poetry collection, revised edition, 2021

A number of poems have been set for piano and voice and performed
Several short stories have been broadcast by the BBC and repeated
The play 'Letters to my niece' performed in Belfast, Holywood Players 1995

COME IN, BOBBY

A collection of nineteen short stories

1980 – 2022

by
Richard Cutler

In the embrace of eighty and beyond

Proofing MJR Hambrook

Overview Ann Cutler

Artwork Tony Hambrook

Front cover Chris Channing

Back cover Zil Shah

Illustration permission from The Marine Society, Lambeth

Presentation and creative display Rachel Clarke

Copyright © Richard Cutler

First published in 2023 on behalf of the author by
Scotforth Books (www.scotforthbooks.com)

ISBN 978-1-909817-49-4

Typesetting and design by Carnegie Book Production, Lancaster
Printed in the UK by Jellyfish Solutions Ltd.

Contents

Foreword vii

1	Ivan	1
2	Roses	7
3	Patrick	13
4	The man who loved sadness	19
5	Zepelin	25
6	A sideways look	37
7	Lamb of God	45
8	Georges Bourdon	51
9	Condition of Sale	57
10	The return	63
11	Great Circle	67
12	Miss Hall	73
13	The Ming Vase	79
14	He was unexpected	85
15	Lizard	89
16	Miss Whitby	93
17	Wolf Tree	99
18	Lady with a dog	103
19	You'd better come in, Bobby	107

Foreword

In the embrace of eighty and beyond

These stories have emerged into the public domain in drip-wise manner, a drop here then a gap and another there. Some have been seen first in *The Writer* the journal of the Society of Medical Writers, some in the Piccadilly Press and in its successor Piccadilly Paragraphs, one in *The Seafarer* another in *The Lady* – I am grateful to their editors. None of these have been broadcast but several have won prizes. One story was extracted from the novel *Four Exits to Smolensk*.

I am dedicating this little volume to all the loving women in my family. My mother's life was a shipwreck. Only for a brief five and a half years during the war did she find happiness. Disaster closed in around her like a pack of dogs. I had the good fortune to spend the war with my Aunt Clare and Uncle Bill in New Zealand. Clare was a woman of imagination and a writer, stories and plays ... I still have a small volume of three one-act plays on my bookshelf. She also achieved local fame by being a very good teacup reader with a devoted and regular following. And my father being a fine journalist, how could I not go down that road ... but it took some finding. Without my wife Ann I would have been a shadow of the person I slowly became.

My sister Anne was a victim of cruel fate to be born with a faulty gene that stopped her growing. Despite being a woman of diminished height she emigrated to New Zealand, worked for the Post Office, bought her own house and had many friends. Jane my daughter is a blessing constantly and we love her dearly, as we do my son Joe's wife Rose, a gifted musician, and our delightful grandchildren.

The whole family with Joe, Tom and Tony are an endless joy, they ground and place me securely in a world that is strange, uncertain, mysterious and enigmatic. I hope this little booklet travels easily in the pocket and eases a dull wait or a tiring journey.

*

❋ 1 ❋

Ivan

He was different from the rest of his family ... they did not embrace him. It was as if an icebreaker split an ice-flow, his father to the right, mother to the left, Ivan between them in a passage of half frozen water. No one knew where he had come from, not until Aunt Lola said there was a distant cousin, Cousin Lobok, who had been shot in St Petersburg in the 1905 uprising. As no college wanted him Ivan decided to educate himself. He returned one day and announced he had become a student near Gray's Inn. His parents sighed relief. The Holborn Reference Library was a college – for many.

They had to wait at the church.

Ivan took from his coat pocket his reading glasses and eased himself out of the crowd. From another pocket he lifted out a book of short stories and gazed with awe at the title, with a reverence reserved for a holy relic. With fingers trembling he began to read. It had a calming effect on him ... a different world – one he could enter. When he raised his eyes his father's coffin had arrived. The priest led the procession and the pall bearers moved forward carefully, in step – men from his father's regiment. The church doors were open wide, the mourners entered.

Ivan slipped his book back into his pocket and joined the end of the file but too late to be with his family. He remained at the back with the gardener, Grigori. Afterwards the family gathered in a large house in Ealing. It was bordered on one side by a wide expansive golf course and beyond a line of willows marking the passage of the River Brent. As the sherry and vodka were passed round Ivan became the subject of discussion and comment. His sister passed around sweet Russian cakes, her brother Mikhail offered vodka to the Russian uncles. Oblivious, Ivan was in another world. He sat on a stool in the window bay engrossed in his book, entranced by the opening story – *The Swedish Match*. He admired, loved, the examining magistrate's secretary – so talented, so observant and insightful, so bold.

It so happened they ran out of milk – tea taken in the English manner.

'Tell Ivan to go. Make him useful for a change.'

He was despatched to the supermarket. Unfortunately, he forgot to pay. Beyond the barrier he was grabbed by security, frogmarched to the manager's officer where in his fright he allowed the two-pint carton to slip from his grasp. It burst open and shed its contents over a new carpet. The manager was outraged and sent for the police. Eventually Ivan returned home without the milk but bearing a summons. His mother was dismayed. The rest laughed till they cried.

The case came before the Willesden Magistrate's Court on a hot summer's afternoon, Ivan presented with his mother. She was still mourning – a long black dress, dark shoes and a curious old-fashioned sun hat. When Ivan was called before the bench the magistrate, a slight silver-haired man, gazed at him across the top of his glasses.

"Are you Ivan Lasky?

"Yes."

"You are charged with stealing two pints of milk, and causing substantial material damage … How do you plead?"

"I am guilty," said Ivan in a clear voice.

"Good. Then we shall not take evidence." The police officer and the store's security guard were waved away. "Are you able to tell the court, Ivan, what exactly happened – you may wish to bring before us some mitigating circumstances."

Ivan hesitated. He blinked in the shaft of bright sunlight coming through a gap in the courtroom blind. The clerk of the court handed him a small leather-bound book saying he must tell the truth and nothing but the truth. But Ivan had become lost in thought.

The magistrate before him was so unlike Tchubikov in the story – he had kind intelligent eyes touched with humour. Absently his fingers went to his pocket and lifted out his book.

"I do."

"What is that book you are raising, Ivan ... something sacred to you? It is clearly not our New Testament."

"Oh ... sorry."

"Bring it here." The magistrate looked at his side members, shrugged and gave a faint smile. Ivan left the dock and walked past the clerk. The chairman took the book and showed it to his side members.

"I see. You are a lover of Chekhov?"

"Yes, sir. I love him very much."

"Really ... do you know where he was born?"

"In Taganrog, sir, in the Ukraine – on January 16, 1860," Ivan hesitated, "Actually that is not certain – some people say in was the 17."

"I see. When do you suppose he died?"

"In Badenweiler on the second of July, 1904."

"Thank you. Quite young. Only forty-four. What did he die of?"

"Tuberculosis ... he had it for many years. Even when he was so ill he managed to write and finish 'The Cherry Orchard' in 1903."

"Thank you. Please return to where you were standing." The bench conferred. After several minutes the chairman addressed him.

"Ivan – you are clearly an intelligent and able young man. The theft of this milk and the mess you made was unfortunate. We still don't know why you did it. Perhaps your mind was elsewhere? However, you have been brought before us because the supermarket makes an example of people found pilfering. We have decided to impose a fine. What you did was wrong. Thirty pounds."

"No, sir."

"What was that, Ivan ... do we hear you disagreeing? This is a fine handed down to you from this court. It is not a request. Nor is it a railway ticket."

"I will not pay, sir – in all due respect for your kindness and wisdom. I shall do community service."

"Oh? Is that so." Ivan looked across to his mother. She was white-faced, dismayed at his audacity. "Then you will be taken down to the cells while we decide what community service we shall impose on you." The magistrate nodded to the court usher. "Take him down and give him a cup of tea. He may read his book."

The three hours in the cell until the afternoon's hearings were over was a pleasant time for Ivan. It was quiet, cool compared with heavy heat outside, and he was given two cups of tea with some marble cake. Eventually he was taken upstairs into the magistrate's chamber – a neat room with a desk, telephone, two easy chairs and a table against the window.

"Take a seat please, Ivan ... one of these easy chairs." Ivan did as he was asked, and waited. "Your mother has been up to see me. It seems that the milk in question was stolen on the day of your father's funeral." The magistrate touched his chin and paused. "I am very surprised, Ivan ... I hope you don't mind me using your first name?"

"No, sir. Not at all."

"That no one in your family saw fit to inform me of this. A note would have sufficed and it would have saved you from all this – the exposure and public reprimand."

"My family believes in punishment, sir."

"Hmm. I shall see that this is not recorded as a crime." A warmer look entered his eyes. "It so happens I, too, am a lover of the Russian masters. What is your view on Dostoyevsky?"

"I prefer it when he is not so serious."

"Quite. And Lev Nikolayevich Tolstoy?"

"A master, sir. I am not worthy to comment."

The magistrate nodded. "However, you have committed an offence and have opted for community service. Report to my house next Monday morning at nine o'clock sharp. You may go."

The following Monday morning was much cooler, showers had blown in on a gathering west wind. Ivan left home early armed with a tube map, a travel card and a ten pound note from his mother. He made his way to Holborn. There he found Mecklenburg Square, walked around three sides of it before finally discovering No. 17B. He pressed the button opposite the name – Professor Kropotkin. A voice. He was told to come up. The door buzzed and opened easily to his push. He entered a cool white marble-floored hall. The magistrate greeted him, led him up a short flight of stairs, through a glass-panelled door and into a gracious high-ceilinged room lined from top to bottom with books. A library. Broad windows flooded the room with morning light.

Ivan was breathless in admiration. "A magnificent library, sir!"

"Thank you. But don't be deceived. These books are jumbled up and in total disarray. Your community service will be based here. You will need to bring about some order – a full inventory – author, title, date published. I also receive daily enquiries. You will man the phone, answer where you can. I am away most days so you will be on your own – bring a thermos and sandwiches. I want you here from 9 am to three. There is a kettle, and a fridge. Later you may need to travel with me abroad."

Ivan went to the books and touched them reverently with his fingertips.

"How long is my community service, Professor?"

"Quite. I shall review your sentence ... from time to time."

*

✤ 2 ✤

Roses

He told me as I was finishing placing the flowers on the window-sill. I had just turned around to ask him if he liked the arrangement, a good place for them. As a boy he used to be very particular where I placed cut flowers.

"What do you think, dear?"

"I have got married, Lydia."

How strange to be called Lydia like that and not 'Mother'. We have crossed a bridge. He is now married and I have become Lydia. He hasn't said if he liked how I had set his flowers, only that he has a wife. He never brings me roses – he knows they make me sad. Perhaps that was why I wanted to know if he liked them there. Perhaps his wife chose them.

"Oh." It was the only word that came to me. Shocked ... yes. Surprised ... very. But mostly I have lost my ability to be surprised ... I am not ageing well. David is coming nearer and touches my arm. It is the touch of a rose ... sweet and sharp. I always bleed when I go near them.

He's left me – gone to the kitchen to make coffee. Memories surge into my eyes – my mother when I told her that Lawrence had proposed to me and that I had accepted him. We were in the kitchen. Kathleen was stirring a saucepan. I had come up from London in the new car Lawrence had helped me choose.

Mother said, "What a thing to tell me, Lydia, when I'm making white sauce."

But she did know him. And she liked him. Who David's wife is I haven't the faintest idea – but that's him. Some things he always kept secret. A lovely boy, but not sharing his heart and mind with me most of the time. All right ... some of the time.

He came in with the tray and brought over Lawrence's coffee table. It's always been wobbly but his father was proud of it. Mother moved her sauce off the light and hugged me, delighted. But am I? Delighted? I don't have her tenderness of heart. My eyes are moist ... memories. I have been saturated in sorrows, and what sad thoughts can well up when you least want them. Not now. Not this moment. My son is happy, so must I be. I am affected by the roses ... roses and marriage, roses and birth – and all the rest. Alone I would have cried and put on the Mozart Requiem. It has always answered me before.

"Shall I bring in some biscuits, Mother?"

One is always a mother when a son asks where the biscuits are.

"In the green tin. I keep them in there now."

"Not the Noddy tin?"

"No."

How can one release a son bearing a lifetime of love, memories, photos into the arms of another woman. He came back in and placed a Bourbon biscuit on my saucer. He has lovely hands. Perhaps his new wife will love them too.

"Nothing will change, Mother. Just three of us instead of two."

Once we were four. Lawrence died, then Peter in the avalanche where he shouldn't have been – on a mountain that hated climbers. Then we were two. But now ... three. He should not have brought me white roses, even if they do have pink markings. I must ask him, mustn't I, about the wedding I was not invited to. He would be hurt if I went now out into the garden. Lawrence always said people must have space to do their own thing. In Russian, he used to say, there is no word for privacy.

"Mother, are you with us? I am married but nothing will change. Stella agrees."

"Ah yes. Stella agrees."

"Don't you want to know about it ... our marriage?"

"Of course, darling. Did you get married in Antarctica?"

"Don't be cross. Peter was the snow and ice man, not me. We were married in Cricklewood last Saturday. You are invited to a small gathering on Sunday at the surgery. Only closest family. They want to meet you."

"Do they? Cricklewood? Your father and I went there on the bus. Do you remember the stamp shop? Daddy used to take you there on a Saturday morning. Such a nice man who owned it, but so sad. Mr David Greenbaum. Fancy me remembering that."

"You're obfuscating, Mother. Listen, I am a married man now. The gathering is in Cricklewood as you rightly guessed. And we don't mind if you bring Doris, or one of your other friends. There will be canapés and champagne."

"When your father and I married we didn't go to Southport like Lawrence's mother suggested. We had our honeymoon on the Isle of Man. Your father had digs in Liverpool and loved the ferries. You were conceived on a ferry in Liverpool Bay. There were always roses on the captain's table. It was so charming. The chief steward only took them away in storms."

"We thought you'd like these special roses. They have stripes."

"They are lovely. From Tesco? Tell me then about your Stella. You weren't always quite so secretive. Is she also a writer?"

"She is Stella McMurdo. An archaeologist. Her father is a GP. They are a Scottish family. Catholics. We were married in a Catholic church. You wouldn't have liked it, Mother. And so many people ... you wouldn't have known any of them. A small gathering seemed more sensible. Stella thought it would be best ... so did Bess."

"Did they? I have no problem with Scots or Catholics. How unusual no one thought to ask me."

"You hate all those crowds, Mother ... and in a Catholic church you would feel very strange."

"I'm not as narrow as you suppose. Have you become a Catholic as well?"

"Stella is a Catholic, of course ... and so are Ben and Bess."

"Ah. And a reception in the presbytery?"

"Mother, you are in a funny mood and irony doesn't become you. I'm telling you about the best thing in my life and you keep coming out with oddities and ironies. If we'd got married in Camden Town Hall you would have been invited. Not to a Catholic church."

"It seems my family is expanding – no Lawrence, no Peter, but a Stella from somewhere beyond the Tweed and a Ben with a GP's surgery, and a Bess who thought the bridegroom's mother would be too embarrassed to come to the wedding. You could have informed me, I suppose, on a Christmas card, or on a postcard from the Seychelles. If I'm upset ... I'm sorry. Is there anyone else?"

My son hesitated. For the first time. "Stella has a ten year old daughter, Molly."

"My goodness. A grand-daughter. Whatever next?"

"You'll love her, Mother, she's very perky and cheeky. At the moment she calls me Uncle David. There's no hurry to change that. Her father Andrew died when she was three. Your coffee's getting cold, Mother. Should I hot it up for you ... another biscuit?"

My son has always had a less attractive side. Furtive. No ... more like secrecy in a harmless way. I have always found that in writers and stamp collectors. They live in three worlds – stamps, imagination, and occasionally in the same world as us. I love him. There are worse things to announce to a mother than a wife and grand-daughter. I am sad. Sad they didn't want me there. Sad they never once told me about themselves. Sad because I feel unwanted and an embarrassment. I must stop. Love is such a fragile thing – it arrives when you least expect it and goes when you least want it to.

"Your father and I were married quietly. His parents didn't come ... we had met on an Aldermaston march and in those days I wore a CND woolly hat and badge. Afterward Lawrence wanted to go to the Isle of Man and he took me there on his motorbike. He adored the TT races. You should go somewhere warm ... with your Scottish Stella."

"We're going in the summer to Venice. Ben has a flat there we can use."

"I suppose he isn't a McMurdo?"

"Dr Keith from Edinburgh."

"A flat in Venice. How your father would have loved that. He admired all things Italian. Always did well in Latin at school. He took it at Merton and could have become a curator of antiquities at the British Museum, had he not chosen to be a writer. So you're like him in many ways." I stood up and kissed him. "Don't mind me – I'm always silly when there are roses in the house." I went to the kitchen for the secateurs and my new gardening gloves. Colonel Rice bought them for me last week when he took me to the garden centre. I prefer my old ones but I'm trying to get used to them. David is standing in the doorway. I hope he is happy. Contrary to what David says and thinks about me, I do have a leaning towards church and all its mysteries. I go most Sundays now – and that is where I met Colonel Rice. He's coming this afternoon, but David won't see him. It's a long drive back to London.

"That's a fine machine, Colonel Rice. A Norton. They often won in the Isle of Man. Lawrence and I often went over … he loved the trials."

"I'm glad you like it, Mrs Brandon. May I tempt you this afternoon for a little jaunt? They do a very good afternoon tea at Highdown House. Quite the best sultana scones. And the Downs are at their very best at the moment."

"Yes. Thank you … but only if you will do something for me."

"Why anything, my dear Mrs Brandon. Name the task. Up for anything."

"Would you mind running me up to Willesden in North London next Sunday? My son's new in-laws have invited us to a wedding feast."

"Really? A wedding do? Fancy that. Both of us?"

"Why, yes. They are very keen for me to have a companion, a friend. I have ridden through France, Spain and Italy on pillion. And once round the TT circuit."

"By Jove. Why then, my dear friend, Willesden it is. What fun!"

※

✤ 3 ✤

Patrick

Mrs O'Clare came home usually about 2.30 pm. Since the onset of her asthma she had been moved out of the loom room into the canteen. And she was glad. Mrs Doherty, the shop floor delegate had taken her to one side.

"Listen, Frances, you are suffering from loom asthma. 'Tis all this fluff and dust over the years. An industrial disease. Should you not put in for compensation like poor Mr Kilby? Doesn't he just get half his money now from London. And if they say no, we'll take it to a tribunal."

But she didn't want any of that. Not now they'd given her the lovely canteen. She opened the front door and called out like she always did.

"Patrick. I'm home."

A deep silence hung in the air. Her voice echoed. On the kitchen table was a note printed in pencil – the pencil she should take back to Father Kenny – printed in Patrick's large letters. GONE TO WORK MAMMY.

She sat down at the table and felt in her handbag for her inhaler. The shock had quickened her heart and made her wheeze. She placed the blue inhaler in her mouth, breathed out quickly like Nurse Nora had shown her, squirted and sucked in the wonderful spray, the spray of angels. She did it again, a hiss and a gulp. Since losing her husband, she had come to speaking to herself in the house and occasionally outdoors when no one was near.

"A job? What in the name of the Holy Mother is that? Sure and the boy's never worked. This is a powerful shock. I shall need some tea."

Mrs O'Clare filled the kettle and with a trembling hand dropped a teabag into her Giant's Causeway mug. "What on earth is happening here? My Patrick is not a working man – the Good Lord never wanted him for that. Not even the Holy Father himself ever suggested such a thing."

When she felt calmer she went next door to see Mrs Doherty. Her neighbour turned off the Hoover and the two women sat themselves down in the kitchen.

"Whatever has happened to my Patrick? Has he not just left me the strangest of notes. And him a boy who never writes. Does he not always wait for me with a cup of tea and a digestive biscuit, Mrs Doherty. Always."

"I saw your Paddy go out, that I did. About eight o'clock, Frances. Sure and I couldn't believe my eyes. That I couldn't. He's never been a boy for leaving his bed."

"And I don't say you're wrong. Mrs Doherty. He always got up when his father was alive. Since his Daddy was taken up he's become a powerful deep sleeper."

"You'll be needing a strong cup of tea, Frances."

Mrs O'Clare took out a handkerchief from under her sleeve and wiped her forehead. "Haven't I just had one, Mrs Doherty. But it is something to settle me I need. That's a fact. That is a fact."

"Then you shall have another. And a little sugar. Doctor Doyle won't mind. Not this time. Sugar for shock. Wasn't I the first aid lady in the loom room for twenty years? I know all about shock."

"That you do, Mrs Docherty. How could I ever know my Patrick had working on his poor wee mind. Of all the things to trouble him, thank Our Holy Mary, that that was not one of them. How did he look ... was his hair brushed?"

"Paddy didn't look any different, Frances. Sure he never brushes his hair except on Sundays."

"He misses his Daddy, that he does. It needs a good man in the house for a growing boy. My Mam always gave thanks we were all girls."

"Mr O'Clare was a great wee man, Frances."

"So he was that, Mrs Doherty."

Mrs O'Clare was restless all day, beside herself with worry, looking at the clock and praying softly on the half hour that Patrick would walk in and that she could prepare a meal – so hungry would he be after a whole day working – working for the first time. By six o'clock she was so agitated she had to go back in to Mrs Doherty. Her friend switched off the Hoover and took her into the kitchen.

"He's not back yet, Mrs Doherty." She said, fear in her voice.

"And I've not seen or heard anything either, Frances. You know how he clumps around."

"You'll not be hearing anything with your vacuum cleaner on every hour of the day, Mrs Doherty."

"'Tis only background. It is so. If I don't hear your Patrick singing it is because I have the looms ringing in my ears, and me retired a ten year gone."

"He's never been out so late before. I can't think what job it might be to keep the poor man out so long. He is not made for working – the Blessed Virgin saw that he had other gifts."

"My husband was never made for work either, Frances. And the only gifts he ever had was the time he won sixty pounds on the Grand National. And now he's getting too old for it – for work."

"You can only have a man around you for so long, Mrs Doherty, then you have to send him out. It's natural. That's how it is."

"You won't be knowing what to cook for him, Frances."

"'Tis a strong broth I'm making."

At 7 pm Patrick did return. He sat down heavily in his Daddy's chair. His mother was so overcome with relief she could say nothing. After drying her eyes, smelling the broth and feeling calmer she came back in.

"'Tis a wee job you have now, Patrick?"

Patrick unlaced his shoes and put on the slippers his mother passed to him.

"It is so."

"You'll be needing some strong hot soup."

"I'll need to wash my hands, Mammy."

"You tear away on."

When her son came back, Mrs O'Clare waited to be enlightened.

"This is a powerful strong soup, Mammy."

"Has it not got a third OXO cube … you'll be wanting strength after all that working. Is it in Belfast you are?"

"It is so, Mammy." Patrick buttered some bread and dipped it in the dark soup.

"And how did you come to get it, Patrick? The Job Centre wouldn't treat you like that, not after all these years, not the kind Miss Monaghan. The sweetest of girls."

"I met the Holy Father and asked to work. He said yes."

Mrs O'Clare crossed herself. "The Holy Father! To be sure the Lord God, the Holy Virgin and the dear Lord Jesus have found you at last." They were both silent. Patrick tipped the bowl and finished the last of his soup. "Can I come with you and see where it is you are, Patrick. For my peace of mind. Holy Father and all, but I am you own mother – a silly, worrying woman. And Daddy would want me to."

Mrs O'Clare asked her friend Moira to stand in for her at work, took the Monday off and made her way to Central Station. She crossed the Lagan Bridge, walked past the new conference hall already looking magnificent and impressive – a gift to Belfast Mrs Doherty said – from Germany, on account of the bombing.

"Where are you taking me, Patrick?"

The boy looked at her with a gaze she thought must have the joy of Jesus within it, and they hurried forward so much quicker than usual. He did not explain. As they drew near to St Ann's Cathedral a disturbing doubt entered her mind – that there were no places around here Father O'Donnell or the young Father Kenny would come to. Her doubts became a panic. He led her up the steps of the great Protestant Cathedral with all its recent restoration – money from Brussels, said Mrs Doherty – a dubious Protestant stronghold with its tentacles into Europe and reaching out towards Rome itself.

Her throat was dry, her heart beating hard and the desire for her inhaler was beginning to take charge. "In here, Patrick. Can this be so? Holy Mary."

He left her and went into a side room in the new extension and brought out into the light of day, his brush and a long handled dustpan. The Dean came over to them.

"This is my Mammy, Holy Father."

Mrs O'Clare was struck speechless, her fingers in the depth of her bag clutching the blue inhaler. She was overwhelmed. The powerful radiance around them, the holiness of the cathedral, the angelic smiles she was receiving. Instinctively and without any hesitation she dropped to her knees, reached forward and kissed the hem of the Dean's cassock.

"God Bless you, Holy Father." And the tears that had sprung into her eyes began to escape down her cheeks. She hurried away in a state of great agitation, pausing only to puff at the blue gift from the Archangel Gabriel and Dr Doyle. When she got home she noticed the net curtain move and the face of her friend beckoning her in. Mrs Doherty placed her arm across her friend's shoulders, just like her Mam used to. Mrs O'Clare fought back a new wave of tears. There were no tears in Mrs Doherty's house – and no dust.

"Did you find out, Frances, where it was?"

Mrs O'Clare lifted up her inhaler and used it for the fourth time. Dr Doyle said she could use it more on a bad day. "He works for the Holy Father, Mrs Doherty."

"Ah. God bless the dear man. Is it a big home, Frances?"

"A powerful big home, Mrs Doherty."

"Is not the Holy Father a great man. So he is. The true shepherd with the lost lamb – more precious to him than all his found sheep. Is that not so, Frances?"

"It is so, Mrs Doherty. He leads his sheep into green pastures."

"And your poor Patrick will now be safe from all those unbelieving Proddies."

"Are we not all God's children, Mrs Doherty."

The two ladies sipped the hot sweet tea quietly – as if an angel had flown past.

✼

❊ 4 ❊

The man who loved sadness

Put it this way, Charlie was at the other end of the party-animal spectrum. So what I'm going to tell you may not sound that odd ... but stay with it. I can say, hand on heart, it took me completely by surprise.

I'd known Charlie for about three years. We first met in whispers. You may think that shaped him, made him the man he was. Whispering, I mean. No ... nothing wrong with his voice ... he didn't have a cold and sore throat ... he worked in silence. When our first encounter took place he hadn't long landed this job in the Holborn Reference Library. I'm talking about a while ago when this was a rule in most libraries. No talking. In fact there was a notice drawn up in large capitals by his boss – a woman I never approached – that said 'NO TALKING ALLOWED.' Well that kind of amused me.

When he came close to my desk I caught his eye and pointed.

"I don't get it ... does that mean no talking at all ... or no talking aloud."

He smiled ... and he was not a smiler. "I'm sorry, sir. It's the rule in here. Miss Heron insists on it." He dropped his voice to a whisper. "It's in my standing orders."

So that was one thing. Not exactly a place of animation and jokes. Like working all day in an enclosed order. An umbrella of silence with a Mother Superior. For all that, Charlie loved it.

But then there was his flat. Sort of flat. A couple of rooms and a little kitchenette annexe. You may say how on earth do you know that ... those people never ask you back home. A typical loner. Correct, but it happened this way.

I bumped into Charlie one lunchtime in Gray's Inn on his half day. You can only wander around in there from 12 to 2 pm. Otherwise it's out-of-bounds to the public. He was carrying two large heavy bags. I had learned his name already. I'm like that – asking for someone's name. It's a spiritual thing. A name, I mean. People like to be addressed by their name. It gives them a sense of being and reality. And it's nice. I think so.

"You've got a right load there, Charlie. Let me help. I can go your way."

So I did. Took a bag. To his flat. Despite what you might have thought, and me too, I was surprised, clean and neat with lift-up beds slotting into a wall behind some oak panelling. It looked out onto a graveyard.

"This is great, Charlie. Here on your own?"

"Yes. Why ...?"

"Makes it harder for you ... with all those graves outside."

"I like it that way."

"Family look in?"

"I have no family."

"Ah." I was taken aback at that. No one in his life. "Bad luck ... so what's your thing?"

"Music."

"Really?"

"I listen to it all the time."

"What ... the radio?"

"Radio Three, Classic FM. CDs. I go to the Proms."

"Really. All of them?"

"I can't afford that. Just special ones. If I can."

"What's special ... Beethoven ... Wagner ... Strauss?"

"Mozart."

"Ah." I shrugged and spread my hands. "I'm glad. What a wonderful counterweight to all that working in silence."

I like music and we got to know each other better. But I like all music – jazz, hip-hop, soul, Bob Dylan, The Who. But I can enjoy a good classical concert. Tchaikovsky ... he's the main man. Anyway one day my girl-friend Sophie says to me:

"Jack ... we're having a thirtieth bash for Julie, my friend ... a party in her flat."

"Great. Go for it."

"She's pretty bad ... upset. Her boyfriend has just dumped her."

"I'm sorry. Fill me in."

"It's stupid and cruel. They were steady. Then he found this woman on the web."

"Well – that's weird. He already had someone ... the man's an idiot."

"Maybe. But it wasn't going well. She's been crying."

"Well ... it happens."

"Julie's seen you in Gray's Inn with a guy ... a tall handsome bloke ... she works around there ..."

"Yes?" I waited. She's looking at me. "OK ... that's Charlie."

"Is he nice?"

I shrugged. "Who can say. I think so. I like him."

"Is he sorted?"

I smiled. I can see the way this is going. "I don't think so."

She touched my arm. "Bring him along on Saturday. Julie would like to see him."

"He's a quiet one. He works in the reference library in Theobald's Road. It's a silent order. Can go the whole day without speaking. If he's lucky a few whispers. It's as silent as a grave. Come to think of it he lives overlooking a load of graves."

"A party will do him good. You can have too much silence and stuff."

"I can't see it."

"Julie will be nice to him. She has a real caring side. And he's good-looking. Anyway, she's a girl who likes a strong silent man."

"I can tell you for sure, he doesn't do parties."

She paused and pouted. Sophie is not a girl to be put off. She has a big heart, and it's for her sorrowful friend ... "Listen, Jack ... the thing is to come to the flat early and put him in the kitchen. There'll be a mountain of rolls to get ready, the drinks to be sorted ... glasses and plates ... those cardboard ones ... sausage rolls to heat up ... and I'm going to buy two dozen samosas ..."

I held up my hand. "He's not some kitchen au pair."

She kissed me on the cheek. "Please ... do it for me. Ask him ... ask Charlie."

How could I refuse. I put it to him ... well not exactly, know what I mean – I told him to meet me under the Francis Bacon Tree in Gray's Inn on Thursday ... his half day. He was there first, sitting on the bench engrossed in an enigma puzzle lost to the world. I took it from him. He had to give this some real attention.

"Charlie, you're wanted at a party." His eyes are widening. I hurried on. "My girl-friend's mate ... Julie. Don't worry ... this isn't a mingling job and all that jokey stuff. They need someone to butter rolls and fill them ... like an hour before the gig. Free beer for you ... as much wine as you want ... no-one to disturb you. You'll be in the kitchen and whenever you want to go there's a back way out down the fire-escape. Go on ... please ... give it a whirl. And there's some great samosas and sausage rolls. You'll need to heat them up ... then help yourself. Think of it."

"I am thinking of it."

"Julie's low. She's just been dumped. She's seen you. It's her idea."

He sighed and reached out for the puzzle. "Sorry. I don't do parties. Not even from the kitchen."

I then came in with the killer punch. "Ah ... but there's a great Hi-Fi music centre in the kitchen. Big speakers ... fantastic sound."

So he came along. I introduced him to Julie and my Sophie and took him into the kitchen. A huge basket of rolls, loads of cheese, tomatoes, olives ... beer, wine ... you name it.

Well to be truthful after that we forgot all about him. It was a great party. I met some cool kids. I mean really cool. Charlie came out from time to time with supplies – the rolls and all ... topped up the beer and wine ... swept up some broken glass. Yet it was like he was invisible. He kept his eyes down, looked at no one ... didn't say a word. And vanished.

About 11 pm suddenly I said to Sophie ... Julie was not in the room ... "Good God ... where's my mate ... I've forgotten all about Charlie. He's vanished. He must have gone home." Then I saw her ... Julie. "Julie! I've forgotten all about Charlie ... where is he ... has he gone?"

Julie touched my hand. "No ... He's in there." She pointed. "In the kitchen. Listening to the Mozart Requiem. I've been sitting with him ... it's wonderful."

*

�֎ 5 ✲

Zepelin

The clapping at the end of the symphony was curious. Rather like the music itself – slow, muted. The shadow arising contained an odour: disapproval. Boris filed out with the audience into a warm night. He lingered on the square watching the leaving listeners become revitalized, as if the hypnotic world they had come from was being shaken off, like a dog emerging from a lake ejecting a water-spray in an uncoiling spasm.

The square cleared. The houses lining it were dark, uninviting, deep in withdrawal. Beneath a curtain here and there, caught briefly and caressed by a southerly breeze, a light showed, a voice entered faintly into the night, echoed upward and disappeared.

Boris approached a door and turned the handle. Locked. He glanced to the left and right – the square was now deserted. A prowling furtive cat crossed from the silent concert hall to his side. The lights in the hall suddenly went off – it became another shadow, an outline lost in the background of a half-lit city, grey-black and unsafe.

Boris took a slender rod from his pocket, slipped the angled bevelled end into the lock and rocked it to and fro against the levers, touching first one then the others, feeling movements within. Suddenly the lock gave, the tongue clicked out of its mortise. He tried the handle for the second time. The door swung open easily. He entered as silently as the shaft of moonlight following him. The house was silent, still.

It felt empty. Boris flicked on his torch and entered the first room from the hall, a space crammed with books. The shelves overflowed and spilled out paperbacks at angles. On the wall were paintings and drawings, each one he lit up momentarily as he swept the beam across the room. Boris, noiseless, silent as a cat covered the whole house from top to bottom. Empty. A small bedroom, a single bed, a rack of pipes announcing the occupant to be a solitary literary man with a thoughtful, artistic taste. He went back down to the first room and shone his torch on a print that, had caught his eye – a Leonardo – St Ann and the Virgin. It had beneath it writing in English. A London gallery.

In an absent moment while still studying the print he clicked on a table lamp by his hand. The room flooded with soft light that fanned out in a pyramid from an amber lampshade. The bureau was unlocked. He lifted down the top and opened a drawer. Empty. He tried several more. In one, an English banknote for fifty pounds. He looked at it admiring its colour and feel before sliding it into his wallet.

He was not entirely surprised to find English money with a print in the house from London. On a broad leather-edged blotter a letter, addressed to 'Alexis Zepelin'. Boris pulled up a chair, took off his gloves, eased it open and read. An invitation to a literary function … guest of honour.

Sounds from outside alerted his senses. Instead of snapping off the light he eased up the desk lid, made his way to the window and drew the edge of a curtain. He cautiously looked down. A shout went up from a sharp-eyed man, one of a group gathered beneath.

"There he is! That's him! Zepelin … you scared rat … come on down … we've seen you."

Boris Ivanov stood transfixed. He stared down into the eyes of the shouting man. Unexplained anger leapt into his throat. He went down to the front door. A sweat had broken out on his forehead. His heart quickened, his jaw tense – he would have to pass through them to get out. The night was lit up like day – the incandescence of flash bulbs. He averted his head. The white glare of the cameras illuminated his profile.

"Alexis Zepelin!" shouted the reporter. "Is it true you've been chosen to read at the Twentieth Congress of Peoples' Artists?"

The aggression of the man aroused Boris's anger further. "No comment."

"No comment? No comment!" A second reporter took it up. "After ten years of silence, Zepelin … ten years dumb … still no comment. Is it always like that with you? Have you nothing to say to all the people who once believed in you? No comment … that is not the growl of a street dog but the whine of lap-poodle, flabby and spineless!"

The man had a cruel face. A cigarette hung from his lips. Even from where he was Boris could smell the reek of vodka. The first man changed the tone – to sarcasm.

"Come on … come on! Not even a tiny little poem for us. You, who once we all admired. Maybe you've forgotten us … and like my friend says, gone dumb. This is a sad day for your beloved country. You see, everyone thinks you are dead."

"I am not dead."

"Ah, the master speaks. The great poet tells us he is not dead. Are we to believe him?" Laughter went through the press men. The sarcasm did not let up.

"Let your people believe it, Zepelin. A poem for tomorrow's paper? Then they will be reassured and may try to love you again."

"Very well. A poem for the rats of the press to float in their vodka, to suck through their soup and spew out into print!"

"Listen. It is the master himself, lofty and showering us with shit from on high. He is right to be contemptuous of his crude comrades."

His colleague joined in. "Speak to us, rats of the press, Alexis. We are waiting in breathless anticipation and awe. Let us hear again our great poet who breaks his silence after ten years with no voice, no courage, hidden away when his own people have yearned for just one line from those cultured lips."

Boris let his rage come out. "Very well." A poem had been echoing through his mind for days. He took a deep breath to distance himself from the taunts and to allow time to enter the words that had invaded his mind. He started quietly.

> "Is today the day that the reaper comes
> to cut a swathe of rye across the sun
> to flush the chiff-chaff to her twilight flight
> and free the white-eyed owl to hunt the night."

Borys elbowed his way through the scribbling group and strode quickly towards the all-night tram.

Next morning in the drab room he rented in a cheap district, Boris woke with a start then leapt from the bed. He reached for his jacket and tugged out his wallet. Still there – an English fifty pound note, worth a fortune in the right place. After a black coffee he hurried to a shop, to a small room at the back and there he changed the precious note for ten times the official exchange rate. A lovely day. His step was light and excited – the very morning for a brisk walk in Gorasky Park, a circuit of the lake and then a good breakfast. For once … a pot of fresh coffee, fresh rolls, ham and cheeses, and today – some chocolate. The day unwrapped in pleasures. The rest of the morning in the city art gallery – there he searched for anything by Leonardo. There was one. Violent – terrified horses within a cruel and savage battle. He walked on taking his time, past the artists of dogma and correctness into a small room of French impressionists. The afternoon he spent in a theatre, the evening in a fine restaurant with many courses brought to him with the best wines. He relaxed and took a paper from the wall-rack. The headline stopped and shocked him. He stared in utter disbelief. There … his photo. A view of himself in profile, hands half coming up to shield his eyes from the flash bulbs. A headline. A chilling headline.

'Zepelin speaks out after ten years of silence.'

Beneath it the story in bold type, front page, his poem. Boris hurriedly returned the paper, paid and left. Back in his room he was dismayed and yet a smile crossed his lips. He got into bed, stretched out and relaxed. What a day. The wine, the fine meal. The warmth. In moments he was fast asleep. He woke at 3 am chilled in terror. Beside him, leaning across him, a figure. A man. His window was wide open. The breeze fanned out his curtains.

"Ah … you're awake now, Ivanov."

Boris backed away to the edge of the bed. "Who the hell are you, for God's sake. What do you think you're doing in my room?"

"I am Zepelin. Alexis Zepelin."

"How do you know my name." Boris shook in fright and fear. His voice hoarse.

"How did you find me ... what the hell do you want?"

"I followed you, Ivanov. We were on the same tram."

Boris was speechless. A deep and terrifying silence. "So?"

"I give it to you, Boris. You have style. You'll go far. Real style. I admire the way you spoke to the press. The rats of the press ... gnawing on your poem and spewing it out in their papers. They got under your skin, didn't they?" The light from the window fell upon the intruder's hand. On a knife. Slim – silvery in the moon's beam.

The glimpse of the knife nearly stopped Boris's breathing. "You want your money back ... well take it. I changed it. There's a lot left."

"Your poem, Boris, is good. So good they think you are me." He gave a soft laugh. "I like it. You have talent. Very good. And just like that ... straight out."

"You liked it?" Boris stared at the man in astonishment.

"Yes. Remarkable." A click – the knife blade slipped back up into the handle. The gleam disappeared. "Don't be afraid, Boris. I haven't come here to hurt you. Your photograph is in all the papers. That is also astonishing. Quite a bit younger – but no one remembers me ... all so long ago."

"You shouldn't be doing this ... breaking into other people's places at this time of night."

Zepelin shook his head. A smile in his eyes. "I like that, Boris. I'm impressed. You have something special. And the whole world now believes that I wrote that little poem of yours. That is real cheek. But I don't mind. The poem is good."

Boris breathed more easily. "So what do you want with me?"

Zepelin put his hand inside his coat and brought out two more English bank notes.

"I've brought two more. Here ... take them. You'll be a rich man now."

Boris shifted his position uneasily. The sweat from his forehead had reached his eyes. He ran his hand across his face. "What do you take me for, Zepelin ... an assassin?"

The man beside him laid the two notes on his bed and flattened them out. "Not an assassin, dear boy. Nothing so crude. I have a proposition. Just right for a man of your gifts."

"What is it?"

"Have you another poem?"

"I have others."

"Good. I want you to go to the Twentieth Congress of Artists in my place."

"What!"

"You'll need to grow a thick stubble and wear some tinted glasses. I'll provide them."

"What the hell is this, Zepelin." Boris's eyes widened. His gaze was on the money.

"Boris … your profile is in all the papers. Of course you must go. No one knows what I look like. You heard the rats of the press … I've not been seen for ten years. You're my height. My hair has a touch of grey but I can easily fix that."

Boris sat up. Alert. "It could be done, I suppose. Is it a trap … why wouldn't you want to go. Why should I help you? It stinks. They were right. You are a bastard."

"No catch, dear boy. Your big chance. Show the world your poetry. And very well paid for it, too. Think of it." He clicked the knife back open. Lifted it. "Of course I could slit your throat, but what a shame that would be … a man of your talent and style."

"Don't threaten me, Zepelin. I'm not a coward like you. And I'm not afraid to speak out. What have I to be afraid of? Not a big man, a one-time star like you."

"That's true. A man unheard of, with no reputation. I shall need to see a poem of yours before I let you speak for Alexis Zepelin."

Boris carefully eased himself off the bed, went to a drawer and rummaged through some papers. "I can't see in the dark. I need the light."

"Put it on."

The room flooded with light. Boris read several pieces then passed a poem to Zepelin, seeing his intruder clearly for the first time. A man not unlike himself – same build, eyes watchful behind glasses, a flick-knife in a gloved hand. A workman's cap covered his head. "Here. This one."

Zepelin took in from him and read it. "Yes, you do have talent. How remarkable. A thief and poet. You are unique, Boris. I like this."

Boris returned to the bed and covered the notes with his hand.

"Not yet. Only one for now." He took away a banknote and slipped it inside his jacket." The one I have will be yours on Saturday. Twelve o'clock. The meeting is at three in the Kaprinski Hall. A car will pick you up from my apartment ... you will need to be properly dressed, with this poem in your pocket. This is a very important occasion, Boris, all our best novelists and poets will be there to listen to you. You must come to my back door and I shall let you in. I wouldn't want to have to come here again." He pressed the knife and the blade retracted." "Like you said, dear boy, who wants to be an assassin. You and I are not violent people are we ... just poets. And one who is about to be famous." Zepelin crossed to the light and snapped it off. In the descending deep darkness he disappeared.

Boris walked slowly to the window and closed it. The dawn had brought with it a chill wind. For some reason his trembling had come back. All that money, a passport to freedom ... get to Kiev. Anton worked on the quays – he would get him a job on a barge.

He approached Zepelin's house as he was told – by the back entrance. The church across the square struck twelve. Deep tones, a solemn bell – a bad omen. He shrugged and was alert, cautious, aware of the danger he was placing himself in. No turning back. Zepelin had left his door open and was seated in an armchair smoking a pipe. The front curtains were drawn. Zepelin's face, half in shadow was impassive. His eyes sardonic.

"Ah ... Boris. I was right – you are no ordinary man." He passed the final fifty pound banknote to him. "Here. You're going to be rich – spend it wisely. Pass me your poem, I should like to read it once more. You'll find some food in the kitchen and some vodka ... if you need it. I've put out your clothes there."

Boris dressed himself in a dark suit and soft English shoes. He put on a striped tie and draped over it a white silk scarf. He gulped down two glasses of vodka and helped himself to the fresh dark bread and sausage. When ready he came out. Zepelin looked him up and down.

"Excellent. You have a little time. Choose a book. Rub this silver streak into your hair. I like the stubble. Put these tinted glasses into your pocket. The lenses are neutral – they won't stop you reading out your excellent poem. I admire it. And so will the literati."

At 2.30 pm there was a sharp rap on the door. Zepelin left him. Boris opened it. He put his hand to his chin – a thick coarse stubble had grown in the last five days. The sunglasses felt good. English, like his shoes.

"Your car is ready, Mr Zepelin."

Boris went out. He sank into the back seat of the limousine. Two men joined him, one of each side and sat close – uniformed men. Thickset. When they reached the hall most of the guests were already assembled. He was helped out of the car and onto a narrow strip of red carpet. At the far end of it, waiting, stood an elderly woman and a tall clean-shaven man in a neat suit, smelling of after-shave. They shook hands with him coolly. It was the man who addressed him.

"Alexis Zepelin – it is so long since you honoured us like this. Your poem in the papers … your absence hasn't dulled your gifts. How have our people been deprived by your silence." Boris shrugged and nodded. "I am the new president, Maximov, and this is my deputy, Madame Fortseva. We both agreed we should start the new presidency by inviting you, hoping you will respond. And you have done. We thank you."

The woman looked deeply into his eyes, her thoughts unreadable. She seemed distant. Detached. As they entered the hall the delegates, writers, poets and dramatists all stood. A subdued applause. Boris was led up to a raised platform, the stage of the theatre and directed to a front seat. The audience became silent. Tension invaded the room. The woman vice-president introduced the proceedings.

"Alexis Dimitrievich Zepelin has told me he has something for us to hear. Is it the product of ten years withdrawal and dismissal of his fellow artists? His brethren comrades?" She slowly extended her hand to the seated guest speaker. "Alexis Zepelin. Please share your poetry with us once again."

Boris stood. He drew the microphone closer, tapped it and spoke calmly and carefully.

"Thank you, Madame Fortseva. If I have not addressed you for many years it is not because I had not wished to do so. Creativity is not like a stream or a tap to be turned on at will." Boris paused – he made that statement because he was aware he had stepped into a pool of danger, and that he had been placed there by Zepelin to save his own skin. Yet the occasion brought a half-smile to his lips. He was rather enjoying the limelight. "I do have a poem, not born in silence or withdrawal." He paused and looked into the audience, into the front row. What a joke. He wasn't Zepelin.

That would shatter the mournful faces of the rigid front row dignitaries. Zepelin had said he had style. Well, let him hear the next bit, or read it in his paper.

"It is an honour, a quite unexpected honour to be chosen as guest of honour to speak to my brothers of the spoken and written word. After music, the greatest art. And an honour to read this work of mine to you." He took the sheets of paper from his pocket. He had rehearsed it twenty times, knew when to pause, drop or increase his voice, when to look up, where to choose a guest whose eye he would find and speak to as if one man to another. He chose a woman. In the second row.

"Fire Spider."

He lingered. A good title … not to be hurried away from. Boris paused and scanned the silent audience. The tension in the hall was now tangible. He broke the silence, his voice clear, rising and falling.

> "Into a white room burnt a minute died.
> The burning flesh smell burned the spider clean.
> A rod of incandescence seared the web
> and scalding downward burned the tissues dead."

He stopped and looked for some moments into the chosen woman's eyes. His words echoed away into a deep silence. He continued more quietly – a less declamatory manner.

> "The spreading red-squat spider fled the fire
> to lurk in caves more deeply mined and fewer.
> No swallow dipping downward saw,
> no fish to suck the swimming spider in
> or mouthing upward suck its shadow down.
> No toppling ant to tangle fast the net
> of red silk vein, no day-lived mayfly
> snare its fragile wing upon the reddened twine,
> no light stunned moth in spiral flutter fall
> to lie entrapped, to scream the spider's bite.
> The red tip burn precedes the blackened knife
> to melt the feeding spider, clawing-cold
> and gel the nest of spider's eggs – dissolve.
> The force that flows to fill the spider's lair
> now sets the mayfly free to grace the air."

A deep silence gripped over the hall, shock held the bewildered audience like a snowfall in summer. A hesitant ripple of applause approached from the back of the hall. It filtered forward, gusting in weak volume. Boris pushed his poem deep into his pocket, gave a slight bow, turned and left the rostrum. At the foot of the steps down the rostrum, two men fell in beside him, one on each side. Close. Touching. They escorted him out to a waiting van. Boris shook them away.

"Don't push me around ... what do you think you're doing. I'm not leaving now ... I have to hear the other poets. Guest of honour. What the hell's going on?"

The van doors opened and two nursing orderlies gripped him and pulled him in. A guard spoke for the first time. Politely. Quietly.

"I am sorry. It was necessary for you to leave now. You have been invited, maestro Zepelin, to attend a clinic, a hospital. Dr Krasny is there waiting for you. It is for your own good. You are in need of help and treatment. Our doctor is the best for your condition."

The applause from the back of the hall had been started by Alexis Zepelin himself. He watched Boris being ushered away, as he had expected – destination not in doubt – the Minsky.

The night train left for Vienna at 5 pm. Zepelin had time to walk to Central Station at a leisurely pace. He chose a back route to enjoy and experience the coolness of the shaded squares, to allow the poem he had just heard to resonate in his mind.

An unknown work-man with a small holdall, a Boris Ivanov, younger looking on his passport, was waved through Security to the express with barely a glance.

∗

❋ 6 ❋

A sideways look

One evening when the stars were luminous, the beach deserted, he had a moment of insight; that he was unemployable. At that same moment Dilip Rao decided upon a career as a freelance – a literary advisor.

With this in mind, he approached a distant relation – seen on occasions in the past with his mother – EV Prasad, who had a pitch outside the Liberty Cinema bookshop, a space he had occupied for many years. Dilip laid before him the following proposition. He respected his uncle, acknowledged his scholarship and was aware that his relative was becoming older. Having undergone considerable self-examination, he – Dilip Rao – had decided that his sideways look could be used to advantage and no longer considered to be a handicap. Taking an overall view, the angle of his gaze notwithstanding, he had decided on a career in literature. But he required a position where his considerable learning – not of course as profound as his uncle's – could be placed before the book-buying public. He was not proposing a job-share, which would be presumptuous, but only to share the site with EV Prasad at times his family member and scholar would find acceptable and convenient.

"Thank you, Mr Rao," said EV Prasad, "it is an interesting suggestion, but you must understand I cannot sub-let my site to any Tom, Dick or Harish."

"I quite understand, Mr Prasad. But you see, like you, I feel I have a vocation. I am a lover of books."

The next morning at 8 am, the Liberty bookshop was quiet – only a few customers buying their morning newspapers. EV Prasad made *namaste* to the Proprietor and asked if he might introduce his relative.

"Mr Patel, this is Dilip Rao the poet … formerly of Cambridge

University. He's made me a business offer, but naturally we cannot proceed with it. We require your approval ... and consent."

Mr Patel noticed the younger man's unusual look. Being a man of rapid thought, and warm heart, he reflected that a sideways gaze was not inappropriate for a Cambridge man.

Dilip hastened to explain. "Only summer school, Mr Patel. I am not a scholar or graduate of the great university."

"I understand, Mr Rao. Even so, summer school is a substantial distinction." He brought them deeper into the shop and waved his hand around in a loving gesture towards his books. "We are quiet at the moment, perhaps you would like to disclose to me the nature of this business matter? Mr Prasad has been advising my customers for years. But if he wishes to take a partner, I quite understand. None of us, alas, are getting any younger."

"I should like to share the site outside your shop with my uncle."

"Ah ... really? You have a little problem with your eyes, Mr Rao, I think?" The proprietor looked away from the young man's angled glance. "You wouldn't be asking for alms, of course."

"Not at all. I have already made out a small card."

"Hmm ... you've given this some thought, I see." He turned to the somewhat detached older man and wondered if he himself was seeing before him the beginning of the diminishing hour-glass. "Would you describe Mr Rao as an apprentice, Mr Prasad ... under your very knowledgeable wing?"

"My young friend has rather sprung this on me, Mr Patel. I don't think he's come to see me as a literary apprentice. We are related, distantly, through his late mother."

"I see. And what does it say on your card, Mr Rao?"

Dilip took a small white card from his shirt pocket. The owner of the Liberty bookshop took it and read it.

"'Literary advisor; and general advice ...' Quite a heady title, Mr Rao. And general advice?" Mr Patel handed back the card. "Some of my customers are from the university, I would imagine most of them would not be in need of 'general advice'."

"I have been a very wide reader, Mr Patel."

"Of course. You would need to be to go to the Cambridge Summer School. You will have to see if your uncle agrees terms ... and then I shall set you a test."

A rental fee was agreed. Sitting times were found, acceptable to both and the following morning Dilip presented himself to the bookshop owner.

"Good morning, Mr Patel."

"Ah ... the junior partner. I see you've reached an agreement with your uncle." With that, he searched beneath the till and withdrew a block of papers. "Here is your test. You may study our stock-list for two days then I shall conduct a little oral examination."

Dilip took the list, said goodbye and made his way home. He climbed to his room, a space with a view on the fifth floor of an older block of flats on the Breach Candy Road. He opened the window and sat on his bed. After a moment's thought, he thumbed through the stock-list then put it aside, taking a sheet of paper from a green cabin trunk under his bed and wrote to England.

'Dear Professor Winthrop,

I am writing to say how much I enjoyed your Summer School. I have now taken a post as 'Literary Advisor' to The Liberty Bookshop here in central Bombay. Should you ever have any enquiries about our writers and poets, please drop me a line. I feel, after such a rewarding summer course, I should like to be of some help to you if I can. We are particularly well stocked with the writings of Rabindranath Tagore.

Yours sincerely and respectfully,
Dilip Rao.

Dilip returned the bookshop's list on the third day as requested. Mr Patel took him into the stockroom. They sat on stools.

"Let us suppose someone asks you for a modern Czech author. Who would you suggest?"

"Milan Kundera. I admire his style and originality."

"But do we stock Milan Kundera?" Mr Patel smiled at him and wondered if he'd ever get used to the young man's sideways look.

"903 ... European fiction."

"I'm sorry about your eyes."

"I have had them since birth, Mr Patel. We are well acquainted with each other. My somewhat oblique look is sometimes mistaken by people who don't know me as a quizzical expression. It has caused me difficulties at times."

"May I try another question, Dilip ... may I call you 'Dilip'?"

"Yes ... of course."

"Who is the current editor of The Spectator?" Mr Patel made a gesture with his hands towards his assistant Miss Majithia – a gentle movement with not a little humour.

"The new editor?"

"Yes."

Dilip gave him the full name of The Spectator's new editor.

"Hmm ... very good indeed. You won't charge me if I come out to you at times ... or send you someone from the shop?"

"Not at all, Mr Patel. Delighted to help."

Dilip took up his place next day and quickly established himself by the depth and breadth of his knowledge. A surgeon from St George's Hospital Eye Department persuaded him to have surgery on his angled gaze, to have the two central cataracts removed at her clinic on Malabar Hill. No charge.

In early December, Dilip returned to his post with clear frontal vision, but he still looked sideways. A mannerism of a lifetime is not jettisoned overnight, he would explain patiently. Mr Patel welcomed him back warmly, took him into the stockroom and made some tea.

"So delighted to have you back, Dilip." He shook his young friend's hand almost with affection. "You have been missed. And now your eyes are better, how splendid. But forgive me for noticing – your look remains the same."

"I find, Mr Patel, I have no understanding of life unless it is viewed obliquely. It is an attitude that I do not think will correct itself."

The proprietor placed his hand on the young man's shoulder. "You are a man with a spiritual life, Dilip."

Several weeks later, perhaps a month – towards the beginning of the New Year – a grey-haired man with dark sunglasses sat down beside him on the cool cinema piazza, took a blue handkerchief from a pocket and wiped his perspiring brow.

"A 'Literary Advisor', Mr Rao …?"

"Yes … I believe I am. To some people. If you have a question or difficulty, I shall help you if I can." Dilip was a little uncertain about this man coming to sit right alongside; it was unusual for a client to adopt such a low position.

"Anything inside by Winthrop?"

"The professor at Cambridge?"

"Yes."

Dilip was aware his visitor was suffering from the heat and humidity.

"Would you like me to bring you a glass of water? We have some cold water inside. Mr Patel keeps it in the stockroom fridge."

"Thank you. That is very kind. I've not been here long – I'm not yet adjusted to these temperatures. Rather too much of a sudden change for me."

Dilip nodded. He wondered if he had ever met the old man before. He brought the water. "Winthrop hasn't written anything for some years. I'm afraid most of his earlier books are out of print. He is in … what shall I say … a period of re-valuation?"

"Kind words, Mr Rao. Dried up, you mean."

"Not entirely. He has a new article in the Times Literary Supplement."

"Ah, you know about that. You are quite an unusual man, Mr Rao."

"Thank you. The title of the essay is 'The influence of Rabindranath Tagore on modern Indian poets'."

"Yes. Of course we do know about you at FitzClare. Summer school?"

Dilip paled and stood up. Professor Winthrop touched his arm. "Please, there's no need to stand. Quite unnecessary. I should be standing – it was presumptuous of me to sit down like that … but I was feeling the heat. Please … sit down here again." The professor continued. "The fact is, Mr Rao, there is a small scholarship you might be interested in for next year's summer school." He took off his dark glasses and laid them on his knees. "That's better. There would be a teaching fee – not very large, they never are – but you'd get all travel expenses and college meals if you wanted them. Have you a subject for me to take back? The printers will soon need it for our brochure. I'm not trying to hurry you but we always like to bring it out before Easter." Dilip slowly sat down under gentle pressure on his arm. "Good … now what's it going to be?"

Dilip looked sideways. A childlike smile of pleasure brushed his lips. "How about the humour of RK Narayan?"

"Splendid." The professor crossed his legs and straightened his back. A young woman approached them. Out of respect and politeness she directed her enquiry to the old man. "Have you 'Ivanov' inside, Babaji?"

Professor Winthrop turned to his colleague. "Have we got it, Mr Rao?"

"916. European Classical Drama. It is not the easiest of plays, Professor, would you say?"

"No, indeed. It certainly isn't. One has to understand the perspective … Chekhov's sympathies."

The young woman shot them a puzzled look, thanked the old man and went inside.

"Perhaps, if you can spare a moment, Mr Rao, you'd like to join me in the film they're showing? The cinema is air-conditioned and it would help me."

The two men stood up and entered the throng of picture-goers. "We may have to take a side seat, Mr Rao, with so many people."

"Some things in life, Professor, are only visible from that direction."

Dilip suddenly stopped and turned. "I shall have to write out a notice."

He hurried back, took a sheet of paper from his pocket, smoothed it out, and wrote: 'I shall be amongst you again soon.'

As he hurried away to rejoin the professor, a deaf, speechless man raised himself onto his elbow, strained his eyes and read the notice. He mouthed the words to himself. 'I shall be amongst you again soon.' He laid himself down again so his back was flat and his head felt the cool firmness of the marble. He concentrated on breathing towards a heart Chakra.

'So,' he said to himself, … 'these are the words of a truly great sadhu.'

*

✣ 7 ✣

Lamb of God

"Don't follow me, boy ... come up here." He had glimpsed and heard the young man behind him for some time. Now he was irritated. The boy hesitantly came alongside the old man. "What is all this ... following me. I am becoming annoyed." He spoke with breaks in his voice – the pull up the hill was making him more and more breathless each week, each month. More troublesome was a recent tightness in his chest.

"Maestro Krasny ... I was only wanting to make sure you reached home safely."

"Why, boy ... why? Am I becoming so ancient I need fussing over? Is that what you think?"

"I often come behind you, Maestro. I'm sorry – today I have been careless." The boy looked down in embarrassment. "We have been worried about you."

"Indeed? And who are all these people who have begun to worry about me?"

"Most of us. The priest ... your congregation."

"I see. You may walk beside me today instead of dancing about behind trees and bushes. And remember this – it is not my congregation. The good people come to worship God and to hear the wise and inspiring words of Father Simic." "Yes, Maestro. But some of us come only for your playing."

Maestro Krasny raised his finger. "Then you should be ashamed ... I am nothing."

The walls of the old country house came into view. Maestro Krasny paused for a second time. He was moved that the boy should be coming behind him to make sure he got back home safely. Not once – but often.

"Well, there it is … my lovely house. Do you know it?"

"Of course, Maestro. Everyone knows *Vanda*."

"What's your name, boy?"

"Anton, sir."

"Yes … you look like an Anton. I love my house, Anton – it is here more than anywhere else that my heart enters my music."

"We all love and admire your music, Maestro Krasny."

"Do you indeed? Are you learning to play an instrument?"

"I play the organ at my own church – St Chrysostom, Jensovice."

"Hmm. Very good. How old are you?"

"I am fourteen."

"Good. And how is it you come to my church to hear me play? Your organist must be too soft with you. Or is he glad to get rid of you?"

"I come on my bicycle. My father is the organist."

"I see … and a very indulgent one. What is his name?"

"Imre Nemec. But he doesn't play anymore. He taught me to take his place. He has arthritis in his fingers and is now a gardener at the Strahov Monastery."

"Then he has three blessings … a love of gardens, a love of music and a son to follow him at his church organ. You may come along further with me."

The old composer pushed open the garden gate. With his arm he moved the boy inside. They entered the seclusion of a wide peaceful garden.

"There, Anton … what do you think? Sit beside me on my bench. We need a rest after a pull up like that. It seems to get steeper, don't you think?"

"It does for you, Maestro." The boy sat beside the composer.

"Can you play any of my pieces, Anton?"

"Yes, sir."

"Then you have a gift. And at such a young age. Do you like playing them?"

"They say, Maestro, that you are writing a Mass."

"Do they indeed. Some more of your inquisitive people?"

"My father was told at the monastery."

"It is true. I am writing some sacred music. Do you think it might be a funeral Mass?"

"I don't know." The boy looked around him with wonder. "What a beautiful garden you have, Maestro. It is so quiet. More flowers than my father's garden. Do you write your music sitting here?"

"Sometimes. We also have a lot of birds. If we watch the bird table you'll see some of them. I put out their breakfast – but a while ago. There won't be much left for latecomers." As they watched a noisy flock of birds, chattering and fluttering descended upon the bird-bath. "Do you know what those birds are, Anton?"

"No, I don't, Maestro. But they seem very happy."

"They are long-tailed tits. You're right ... they are happy birds and flit about chattering, never still. We don't see them very often – this must be a special day, that's why they've come." He smiled and nodded. "Tell me, have you ever played any part of a Requiem Mass?"

"Some of the Verdi Requiem. My father taught me."

"Ah ... really. That one. And what does your father think of it?"

"He says it is too operatic."

"Yes? And you? What's your opinion?"

The boy hesitated. It was not easy to disagree with his father. He looked down.

"I like it, Maestro Krasny."

"Good. It is beautiful. You must ask your father to hear the beauty in it. I am writing a *Stabat Mater*."

A short elderly woman approached them from the house. Anton stood up.

"Slava ... you have a young visitor?"

"Yes. His name is Anton. I have told him I am writing my *Stabat Mater*. He tells me that everyone in the monastery knows."

She lightly touched her husband's forehead. He was hot and flushed. "I'll bring you both some lemonade."

"Bring it to my music room, Anna. The boy plays my music."

He took Anton's arm, led him through the kitchen and dining room into a large room filled with sunlight and a cooling breeze from open French windows. A score was propped on the piano.

"Sit down at the piano and play what I have written."

Anton sat before the score. "Play from where, Maestro?"

"From the beginning of the final chorale."

Anton turned back several pages. "It is not finished yet, Maestro?"

"Of course it's not finished. Anyone can see that. The music in my head has stopped. I may die before it is finished."

Anton began to play. The old composer leaned back into the cushion of his armchair and closed his eyes. The music stopped. "Well then – tell me what you think, boy."

"What I think, Maestro?"

"You heard me, boy. What do you think of it?"

Anton bit his lip. "I don't like the opening."

"What! You don't like my opening. Am I hearing you correctly, young man? You don't like the opening of my finale?" His voice rose.

"With respect, Maestro, I wouldn't open with strings and horns."

"I have heard everything now. So you wouldn't, eh? You are telling the Maestro you don't like the opening to his *Agnus Dei*? I can't believe my ears! Anna ..." He shouted. "Anna ... where are you?"

His wife appeared; flustered. On a tray she was carrying a jug of freshly-made lemonade and two glasses. "Slava, whatever is it?" She attempted to pacify him.

"You're red and hot – you must have some of this cool lemonade. You're upsetting yourself."

"Of course I'm upsetting myself. This boy has just told me he doesn't like the opening to my *Agnus Dei*!"

"Really!" Anna pursed her lips with vexation. "That isn't very nice."

"Nice? It's a confounded cheek." He stood up, went to the piano and placed his hand on Anton's shoulder. "So ... no strings and horns ... perhaps there's something else you object to, boy?"

"Yes, Maestro. I would rather it was in a minor key. D Minor."

"What!" He did not explode but shrugged and looked at his wife, shaking his head. She narrowed her eyes and looked severely at Anton.

"Who is this boy, Slava?"

"Anton is the organist at St. Chrysostom. He wishes me to open in

Mozart's key. Now boy, you'd better tell us what you'd do next. We are listening."

"I would slow it down, Maestro, to andante."

Maestro Krasny poured two glasses of lemonade from the frosted jug. He then raised his hands towards Anna. "Can you believe this. Now he says my *Agnus Dei* is too fast. He doesn't like strings and horns and says it is in the wrong key. Just tell me this, young Anton – who is writing this section, me or you?"

"It is all your music, Maestro Krasny."

"I am relieved you think so. Very well. Anna and I will hear your ideas. You may have this glass of lemonade first."

"We could open with pianissimo bassoons and cellos."

"Bassoons? Pianissimo … you mean with a mute?"

"Rising scale of D Minor." He hastily gulped down a mouthful of lemonade. His throat was dry, his heart beating fast.

"Yes, boy … then what?"

"Two octaves above them clarinets and oboes. Descending arpeggio in the left hand, softly."

"Not together, boy – not together … a third apart. Clarinets above the oboes. And the voices?"

"Altos softly with the melody." Anton sung quietly.

Maestro Krasny pulled a fresh page of manuscript and marked it rapidly.

"C Minor, boy, it is an impertinence to use Mozart's key. Now, move over … give me some room." He sat on the long piano stool beside Anton and set the new score in front of the old one.

"Let's try it," He played the new opening. "Like this, boy?" "Yes, Maestro." "Now … clarinets and oboes like we said. You were thinking of something like this? Or – wait a minute … this?" He wrote quickly and stopped. "No … none of those – what we're looking for is this … don't you agree?" The old composer smiled, played and sang. "Come on now … I can't do the altos. It was there, wasn't … all the time. We both knew it, but you heard it first. Now we're off … cellos and basses with your bassoons. … and your altos."

Maestro Krasny wrote quickly leaning close into the score, marking it with his sharp pencil. "Yes, yes. Now Anton, just listen to this. I knew it was there, it just needed a bit of unlocking." He played and sang. Above him came in Anton with the alto melody.

Anna left quietly. The glasses of lemonade had barely been touched.

*

❊ 8 ❊

Georges Bourdon

Monsieur Arnaudet took the wine bottle from his uncle.

"Sisters … now there's a mystery for you. Men can never comprehend that relationship." A silence had fallen upon the wedding guests. "And when they're from the mountains …" He paused, and looked towards the fire. "I was living once in a village. I shall call it Vivarais – memories are long." He pursed his lips and placed his gaze on the group gathered around him. "Tonight I want to tell you about two sisters … yet I have some reluctance, the ladies listening may be offended."

The woman nearest him, past the softness of youth, tanned and wind-lined, turned to her daughter. "Monsieur Arnaudet will not shock us, Yvette. What can he tell us that we haven't already heard, that we haven't seen for ourselves?"

Her daughter spoke up. "Yes, please go on, Monsieur. Who were these two women?"

"This is for us to hear tonight after a wedding and love we hope will endure forever – a story about two sisters, a silent man and a childless couple. The mayor of Vivarais and his wife Arnette had been married for fifteen years but never blessed with a child."

An older woman close by, Madame Vaudois, interrupted. "I feel for her. I know about that."

"Picture Vivarais – a summer's evening … two young women arriving from a mountain village looking for work. Of their past we know nothing – they are close. Like twins."

The mother of Yvette said, "Life is hard up there – who wouldn't come down if they had the chance."

He looked at her and resumed. "Emilie is the older one. She's taller, slower and pretty in a dark gypsy way, but her looks are diminished by a

severity in her manner and in her glance. The younger is Natalie – quick, small, agile like an acrobat, laughter on her lips – but she can be quiet. Quiet as a mountain in winter."

"Yes," called someone from near the fire, "that's how they are in the Cévennes."

"The mountain had laid its shadow on them, cut into their hearts, eyes and skin – pitted by grit blown from the scree, engraved by winter's ice. I'm telling you these details so that you will understand. They have walked down with all their possessions are in one bag." Monsieur Arnaudet had a half smile on his lips, but his eyes were distant. He paused while the wine was passed from hand to hand. The wood stove gave out a glow into the room. Children near it slept.

"It is time I brought Georges Bourdon into this story. He enters the lives of all three women, the sisters and the mayor's wife." He spread his hand as if outlining a place. "The village of Vivarais was in that part where the Loire is still only a fast stream but it swells to a real and dangerous river in the spring snow. The nearest station is Le Puy, a day's walk away. There is a bus … sometimes. Picture a man upon whom an inexplicable silence has been laid. This is not a chosen mannerism or some form of mutism, this is something strange passing down through the male side of the family, his father and grandfather – beyond that no one knows. This is the deep silence that is known and practised by Trappists. The man lives with his mother who rules him unmercifully, yet for all that, he loves her very much. She accepts his silence – it was in her husband, but less. Georges Bourdon is strong and she admires that; he is also much lighter than her in colouring – eyes a grey-blue like a clearing summer sky when the mist lifts. He has sharp eyes, sees everything, and some things inaccessible to others. Here is a man you will say of no ambition, who asks little from life and expects nothing."

M Arnaudet paused and raised his glass to the table lamp beside him. He swirled the red wine in his glass watching it climb and fall from the sides. "Yes. Wine loosens the tongue – but it never made Georges speak out. This man has a silence upon him as deep as midnight. But then … suddenly … his mother dies." He looked up. The women were following him closely, deeply involved – some of the men had drunk more and were dozing. "So, what happens to this deep, inward man? Does he grieve? Would he weep and cry out in rage towards the mountains? Or is his silence even more choking, locking his lips forever? For the first time in his life he is left with an empty house. What would he do? Use your imagination." He refilled his glass and passed the bottle to his cousin who took it from him without an answer. Madame Vaudois spoke for the second time.

"What could he do in a silence like that? He would be grieving for his mother in his own way." A young woman rejoined them after moving her child further from the wood stove.

"He is a man. He would want a woman."

But Madame Vaudois shook her head. "Everything is simple when you're young, Denise, when you have a small child. No, he would do nothing. His mother is still there. Her spirit is in the house. Her shadow will reach out for him always, for the rest of his life."

M Arnaudet lifted his glass, looked at it, then put it back down. "Georges Bourdon saw the older sister Emilie and asked her to marry him. She agreed."

"There you are," said the young mother, "what did I say. He needed a woman like they all do. I'm not too young to know that."

"The day after the wedding, the younger sister, the quick bright one with the lightness of spirit, came to join them – to live with them ... Natalie. She found a job working in the *Hotel de Ville* for the mayor's wife, Madame Ibert. It was a sad house. There were no children in it. A child for the Iberts would have completed their love. And after three years no child had come either into the home of Madame and M Bourdon. Natalie told her sister how the same thing had happened to her employer Madame Arnette, and the hearts of both women went out to her.

One day Emilie called her young sister to her. "I have decided to go to Cheylard and bring down our donkey. When I am away I want you to sleep in my bed beside my husband." She was away for ten days. Emilie brought down a female donkey called *'Modeste'*. It had taken her so long because the donkey was wilful, stubborn and at first had refused to come. Yet the animal settled very easily into its new life – a more gentle, docile creature was never seen.

And when the pregnancy of the younger sister became obvious to all, the village shook its head knowingly. It was at that moment a strange and bewildering thought entered the head of Madame Arnette. The baby was named Phillippe. There was no silence. He inherited his mother's charm and easy ways. The young child brought the blessing of laughter to that old silent house, and Georges Bourdon loved him dearly. When he was four, Georges built a little seat for him in the cab of his truck. He drove the little boy everywhere, showing him the whole of France." M Arnaudet looked up. The women were watching him intently, their minds quicker than their men. He continued.

"One day when Phillippe was five, his mother Natalie was approached by her employer Madame Arnette.

"Natalie … how old do you think I am?"

"Madame?"

"I am thirty-eight."

"But you look so much younger than that, Madame Arnette."

The other women touched her hair. "There are already some grey hairs, Natalie."

"It's a shame you didn't have a child, Madame. Everyone knows you're a mother at heart."

Madame Ibert smiled uneasily. "Yes. But then … it's not too late, is it? I was pregnant once, Natalie. I have never told anyone that before but I trust you.

Monsieur Ibert doesn't know. It would have hurt him to know. We keep on trying and hoping, but we are always disappointed."

"I understand."

"You fell very easily, Natalie."

"Emilie asked me to."

"Did you find it offensive?"

"Not at all, Madame."

"You are both from the mountains, from Cheylard. There are things you are more easy with than we are from the town."

"We both love Phillippe like a son. He says he has two mothers."

Madame Arnette blushed. "Of course, it wouldn't be possible for me like that. I mean ... if Emilie went up again. It would be unthinkable."

The next day Natalie approached her sister as she was bringing in hay for *Modeste*. "Emilie, isn't it time *Modeste* had a companion. She must feel lonely sometimes. Perhaps you could find another donkey at home?"

Her sister threw down the hay at the donkey's nose. "You have Phillippe, Natalie. One child is enough."

"Of course, Emilie. We both love Phillippe. He is enough. I'm not asking for myself."

"Who are you asking for?"

"Madame Arnette."

"What!" Emilie's brushing of the donkey's coat became more vigorous.

"She's thirty-eight. Her husband cannot give her a child. She wants a baby and it's not too late yet, but it soon will be."

"Has she asked you?"

"How could she?"

Emilie put down her brush and stroked the creature's head, rubbed her neck.

"Do you want a friend, *Modeste?*" She looked long and hard at her younger sister. "Very well. You may ask Madame Arnette here while I'm away. Just for this one time. Only once. Never again."

Emilie was away only for eight days. There were no donkeys to be had in Cheylard. She had to walk on to her cousin's farm 25 kilometres away in Gévaudan. When she returned with a grey male donkey, Madame Arnette kissed her on both cheeks and returned to her husband. The new donkey was called *'Maurice'*. At first *Modeste* barely tolerated him. Later they became inseparable.

"Imagine," said M Arnaudet, "the joy in the mayor's house when her husband discovered that at last his wife was pregnant. Nor did he ask where she had been staying while he was away – a cousin's perhaps. The baby was called Jacques. As Jacques grew up, two things happened. The little boy became devoted to M Ibert, and as the years passed, a deep and strange silence settled upon him.

When Jacques was eight, Charles Ibert returned from Paris after spending a week with his mother. They had spent many hours talking about the boy and his deepening silence. The old lady was a kindly and wise woman. She reassured her son saying he must not worry and that the boy was almost certainly gifted. She gave him to take back for her grandson a half-size cello. M Ibert called the boy to him and said he would be learning it with the *curé*, Father Antoine – a fine musician and cellist.

And the grandmother's intuition was right – her grandson was gifted. By the age of ten he was playing in the department youth orchestra. At sixteen he gave his debut concert in Le Puy, playing the cello concerto by the Englishman Edouard Elgar. Sitting at the back of the hall was Georges Bourdon. Three rows behind him on an aisle seat was Madame Arnette Ibert, the boy's mother. After the concert, Georges Bourdon stood up and left the hall. As he passed Madame Arnette, she saw tears falling down his face. She reached up and touched his arm. Their eyes met."

M Arnaudet emptied the bottle of wine slowly into his glass. A musician picked up a fiddle and played. The melody was slow, beautiful and filled with sadness. Madame Vaudois crossed to the wood stove and spread out her shawl. She gently moved the legs of a sleeping child and lay down. Her voice was quiet, almost as if she were speaking to herself.

"Who can understand the human heart?" She closed her eyes. Sleep approached and enveloped her. "Or the feelings of a silent man."

*

✤ 9 ✤

Condition of Sale

"It is very good. I like it." Sextus spoke to himself. "This is what I want. What I have been searching for. It is here ... everything. They will grow in this place."

The whispers drifted away in the cool airs of early morning, a breeze that fanned a coolness onto wide empty land that faded to sky.

Erica watched the man. He was tall for a Roman, almost as tall as her husband had been. One of the man's eyes was deeply scarred, puckered. Sightless. She had seen him at first from her father-in-law's hut and had followed him as he crossed their land, watching him as he gazed this way and that, turning his head in a curious manner. And she heard strange sounds, grunts, whispers, though there was no one to listen to him. He had not seen or heard her and was quite unaware he was being followed, by a woman ... near him.

The summer sun had risen obliquely across the hillside. It lit up the Roman's white, blue-braided tunic, illuminated his hair, changing it from grey-white into a softness flecked and edged in amber. Suddenly he heard her.

The man stopped and swung around, defensive, his hand dropping onto his dagger.

Erica approached him out of the sun. The Roman screwed up his eye and lifted his hand, setting it against the sun, tense, fearing an attack. A woman. He allowed his fist to fall loosely to his side.

She stopped ten paces from him. She was curious ... a Roman? She scanned him with the gaze of a Briton, suspicious, wary – yet intrigued.

He waved his hand across the hillside, then pointed along the ridge and downwards to the goat field at the foot of the slope.

"It is good. I like it." He spoke quietly, with no accent – she waited.

"I want to buy this land ... from over there." He pointed to the bent wayfaring tree stretched flat and leaning off the wind, its flowers dense as if covered in snow. "To there."

The buzz of bees and the tree's scent reached them as the morning breeze moved off the summit. He indicated the end of the ridge where the land fell away to scree and cliff. "And down there as well." The man pointed to the two fields beneath them. One was the field for their two goats. "Please tell your master, I would like to buy this land."

Erica lowered her eyes. The man's scarred face disturbed and disconcerted her. She was unable to reply to his face.

"No veterans have ever settled in these parts. There is nothing here for you."

The Roman bowed. "Thank you. I am not a veteran – I am Sextus Quinctillius Varus."

Erica returned to the house, helped her father-in-law out of bed and gave him breakfast. "There was a Roman on the hill today, father."

Aeldred drank the thick goat milk honey. He softened the block of bread in a beaker of mead. He did not look up. "What did this Roman want?"

"To buy some of your land."

"What for?"

"He's a veteran."

"There are no veterans anywhere around here."

"I told him so, father."

The old man looked up at her. "What does this Roman look like, Erica?"

She thought, and remembered. "He is tall, becoming old. His face is scarred and he sees only with one eye. He wears a dagger and a white tunic with a blue ribbon around the edge." She hesitated. "And is courteous."

"A Roman?" Aeldred wiped his lips on the back of his hand. "Will he kill us also, Erica?"

"No, father. He is a peaceful man."

"With a dagger? Find out some more. I detest all Romans."

"Yes, father. I will speak to him again."

The Roman did not return for several days. But then she saw him in the goat field and on the slope of Tree Hill, testing the ground. He drove down his dagger and lifted the earth, smelled and tasted it then spat the soil from his lips. The goats came to him. From a flaxen sack he produced a brush and kneeling beside them brushed first one and then the other. At the islands of green he felt with his fingertips for dampness. After observing him for some time, intrigued and puzzled, Erica approached him.

"I have spoken with my husband's father."

Once again the centurion spun around, embarrassed at having been studied. He wiped his dagger tip clean on the palm of his hand and instinctively ran his finger across the blade to see if it was still sharp. A flush had risen to his face.

"Thank you."

Erica was aware of his discomfort and shyness. The gentleness in his movements pleased her. "He has instructed me to speak with you."

"I am ready for your questions. But I shall need to know your name."

"I am Erica. Of the family Cerdinga."

"Does your husband …?" The Roman stopped. There was no husband.

"In our dealings for this land, please address me as Sextus."

"Why do you want our land?"

"For vines. And I wish to build a villa." He paused. "Is there water here?" His face eased into a smile. "Of course – you know I have seen signs of water."

"There are springs."

Sextus detached his dagger from his belt and passed it to Erica. She took it and gazed in wonder at all the jewels inset into the silvered hilt, the delicate engravings, whirls, loops and scrolls – in a corner some tiny lettering. She handed it back.

He shook his head. "No, please take it to your husband's father."

Erica looked at him in disbelief. "If it is your wish. Is it a gift?"

"Yes. What need have I of a weapon now?"

She looked down. "I will, if that is your wish."

"Yes. Thank you?"

"My father-in-law is old. His son is dead."

Erica laid the dagger on the table by Aeldred's wine and bowl. She wiped his face with a soft cloth soaked in spring water and helped him into his cloak and sandals, tied the sash. Taking his arm, she sat him at their table. He stared at the dagger, picked it up and held it into the morning sun. The jewels flashed red, turquoise and emerald.

"What's this doing here?"

"The Roman wishes you to have it, father."

Aeldred eased it from the hilt and felt the keenness of the blade, checked the balance, its feel. The dagger sat neatly into his palm. He replaced it slowly.

"Who is this Roman?"

"A very gentle person, father. Sextus Quinctillius Varus, former centurion of the Fourteenth Legion."

"I know the *Martia victris,* I am not a fool, Erica."

"No, father."

Erica hurried back to the hillside. The Roman had gone. Days passed, a week – suddenly he was there. She ran to him this time. "My father wishes to see you, Sextus Quinctillius." Her words were hurried. Breathless.

Sextus smiled at her formality and followed to the house.

The hut was entirely surrounded by vegetable plots except for one enclosure containing a pig, and beside it some rabbit hutches and a pen of young goats. As they approached, the kids lowered their heads, pawed the ground and sprang into the air.

The hut smelled of fresh rushes on the floor, of lavender and lemon balm tied to the cross beams, and of clean sun-dried linen. Aeldred was seated on a bench. He stood up to greet his visitor.

"Will you sit beside me?"

Sextus sat next to the frail white-haired Briton.

"Bring me the dagger, Erica." She brought it over to them. He looked into the face of the Roman. "You wish me to have this dagger?"

"I do wish it."

"Whose dagger was it? Before you received it?"

"My father's."

"And before that?"

"His father's."

Aeldred stood up and walked slowly to the door of the cottage. He drew back the loose screen which had fallen in front of the door-way. "This is my land, Sextus Quinctillius. Before that it was my father's. It should have become my son's. He fought with the Iceni in the East, and died for it."

"I am sorry. I also lost a loved one there. My brother."

"My father's spirit and his father's spirit are in this land. I shall not sell the love that came down to me." He steadied himself on the door-arch and looked back, his eyes narrowed by the sun and seeing only the Roman's outline within. "Will you take some goat's milk and honey?"

Erica brought a bowl to Sextus. She stirred the honey into the warm milk. Aeldred came in from the strong sun.

"I would not be pleased with you, Sextus, if you were my son."

"Why not, Father?"

The old man smiled at the form of address. He was not displeased. "You are giving away your father's spirit, and that of his father – your grandfather. It has been given into your care from hands that held it in battle."

"I carry my father's spirit within me."

Aeldred returned the dagger. "And yet, I am pleased with your gesture. Return it to your belt." He took an ash rod from the old wine amphora that stood by the door. "I must feed my rabbits. You may negotiate with Erica for the land over there. As from now it is hers." He nodded as if his thoughts had become distant. He was remembering his son. Grief rose into his face. He left with a sigh. "A father should not live longer than his son." Suddenly he stopped and turned back. "Sextus, if Erica were to give you some of my land, what would you do with it?"

"I would grow vines and make wine."

"Bring my chair here, Erica, I need the sun to warm me. I feel cold." He sat down and said nothing for some time. "Don't you know that the fields at the foot of Tree Hill are a frost pocket? Hasn't Erica told you?"

"I shall plant the vines on the hillside, Father. Perhaps Erica will help me?"

The old man shook his head, humour had entered his eyes. "And where do you plan to live … under a tree? Like in your army days?"

"I shall build a villa."

"And will my Erica help you with that also?" The Roman flushed at the taunt. "Who Sextus will live in your fine villa?"

"I would be pleased if you would both live with me there."

"Indeed. It may not please us!" The old man began to laugh. "What about my pig?"

"Father!" interjected Erica, "Father, please. Sextus is sharing our table."

But the old Briton did not stop. "And should we become Roman slaves? You Romans seem to need them."

"You would become my family."

Aeldred left his chair and returned to the bench beside his guest. "That will be impossible."

Sextus paled. "Why, Father?"

"A condition of land transfer."

"I don't understand."

"You will have to become my family."

Erica took each of their hands and brought them together, as if sealing the matter.

Or something else.

*

❉ 10 ❉

The return

The narrow paved edge of the track might once have been widened as a passing place for a carter or sheep, for pilgrims or a detachment from a Roman legion. I paused there in that broader space of the upland way to allow two men on mountain bikes to hurry through. I raised the left arm in a Romanesque manner and bid them well. My days of hurrying have long since gone. Time and I are friends not competitors.

I was in no hurry to move down to the town beneath me. There still remained a distance between us softened by a morning mist. Everything down there seemed in miniature, as did my past. No longer important. A path from the ancient bridle way fell down sharply into a valley. I set off, not without the apprehension all returning travellers feel coming back to a former life and the starting point of departure. I entered a tranquil landscape that helped and settled me – a stream, an old hump-backed bridge with willows and alders all around, sedge in the marsh where the winter floods lingered beneath the surface. The path cobbled in places and slabbed with broken pavings here and there led down to a gate, the unmarked lane beyond and a seat.

I had seen her from higher up. She hadn't waved though she must have seen me too – no one else coming down from the Ridgeway. It was impossible for her to have been there, quite impossible – I hadn't said I was coming back. My daughter and a dog. Not one I'd seen before. As I drew closer she stood up and came through the gate to meet me, the dog at her heels. I spread my hands. We did not embrace.

I was the first to speak. "Whatever are you doing up here, Abby?"

She took my hand but made no answer, offered no explanation. Only a sigh. Tears in her eyes. It shook me. I placed my arm across her shoulders.

"It's all right. Everything's all right."

She shook her head. "Is it, Dad? Are you sure?"

"Yes, I believe so." Such a mystery, her being there for me. "How could you be there waiting for me? How could you have possibly known I'd be coming this way today?"

"It's the only way you come to us, Dad."

I called the dog to me, patted its head and stroked the soft hair behind the ears. "New dog? Don't remember him … seems a fine chap – gentle nature."

"He's Bruno."

"Really … but he's black."

"St Bruno, Dad. Your pipe tobacco."

"Well … that is something … to be named after the contents of a pipe. But rather nice. Thank you." She reached forward and held my hand. Squeezed it. We walked on together down the lane.

Back in the house I felt uneasy. Strange. My two grandchildren – Abby's boys – glanced at me but made no contact, no comment, no question, no hello. I meant nothing to them … they wouldn't have any idea who I was. A tramp more like. There were no photos of me anywhere, name not mentioned, someone who was but is no longer.

My son-in-law has no time for me. Abby took me upstairs to the office. Two men there – one at the computer the other at a broad desk covered with papers, drawings and designs. The man at the computer looked up.

"Hallo … what are you doing back here, George?" He turned to his colleague. "Do you know George, Trevor … my wife's father?" The other shook his head. "He's a rare one … bird of passage." He returned his gaze to me. There was no friendship or welcome in his look. "So what is it this time, George? Come back for something?"

"Yes. I'd say so."

"What?"

"Nothing much … Nothing definite."

"That's George for you, Trevor. Nothing much, nothing definite. It's his mantra. Means we won't lose anything."

My daughter and I went back downstairs. She sat with me at the breakfast table.

"I'm sorry about Bob. You made the house over to me. I think he feels left out."

"Is that a new partner?"

"Trevor is our design and lay-out editor, and does all the artwork. Bob hasn't made him a partner yet. He comes three times a week and teaches part-time at the tech."

"Business doing all right?"

"These are hard times, Dad." She touched my arm. "Can I do you some breakfast?"

"Just a coffee will do, dear." I wasn't hungry. "I don't recognise the boys now."

"You've been away a long time. They don't know you either."

"Your mother?"

"She's still working at the hospital X-Ray department. They like her. Grace's good at her job. I can't see her moving on from there."

"She's got someone?"

"Yes."

"Is he all right?"

"The boys like him. He's the pro at the golf club."

"Ah … then he'll teach them. That'll be a good thing."

She passed me the coffee. And with sugar in it. She remembers. "Where are you now, Dad. I need to know. The last place sent my letters back."

"I've got a job. Permanent. I'm the residential gardener at the Littlemore Hospital. There's a nice cottage in the grounds that goes with it. Suits me. I thought you should know. I am settled now. I'm sorry it's taken such a long time."

"Isn't that a mental hospital?"

"It was. Things have changed, though patients still help me in the gardens. I'm happy there."

"God be praised."

"Indeed."

"Then I can drive over with the boys and visit you?"

"If you want to."

"Do you need anything from here, Dad? Today?"

I shook my head. "A few minutes in the garden on my own. Is my old deckchair still there?"

In the garden, in the warm morning sun, I took out my pipe and filled it. A calmness surrounded me. The house has lost its threat. No fear remaining. After some time I stood up, took some secateurs from my pocket and went up to our old Peace rose. I took three cuttings, placed them in a damp tissue and secured them in a plastic bag. I let myself out by the back gate.

At the seat near the Ridgeway where Abby had met me I stopped and looked back down. It seemed almost as if I was looking back on the life of another person, to a town I had travelled through blindly. We cannot repair what's been done, only ask for forgiveness. The way ahead was bright and the slopes alive with colour in the full sun. The way along the ancient path was timeless, calling me on to take my new journey to its end. My steps seemed lighter and quicker, my shoulders no longer weighted down by memory. I touched the Peace rose cuttings. It is strange how and when peace arrives – it is like love … when it is looked for it isn't there, and when not expected, it arrives. And surrounding this day is an enigma. Why was my daughter waiting for me on that bench? I had told no one I was coming.

*

❋ 11 ❋

Great Circle

In winter the great circle course from Liverpool to St John New Brunswick enters the Greenland icefield at 58 N. 45 W.

The 'Orford' lay at buoys off Gravesend in the middle of a hard winter eight years from the end of a war she had, against all odds, survived. But her life now was drawing to an end – rusted, little money spent on her upkeep, a tramp steamer on her last charter, a full cargo of ammunition from Woolwich Arsenal. After unloading in Canada she would sail on to Yokohama to be broken up. She had a curious name in Dock Street – a vessel strangely blessed and one of the few ships to return from Murmansk. She had come through typhoons, hurricanes and a drunken Russian pilot who smashed her into a quay and stove in most of the foc's'le. She had even received attention from pirates but they withdrew thinking on a closer look she was virtually worthless.

From the foremast yard she flew the red burgee 'B'. 'I am carrying explosives.'

On a grey, ice-misted night in January, loaded down to her North Atlantic marks she took on board her Trinity House Pilot, slipped her mooring chains and pushed forward into the slack black water of Gravesend Reach. She wallowed her way up the North Sea in a stern quarter swell, rolled and pitched herself into and through The Minches. In the early hours of the third day she picked up the Liverpool pilot.

In Birkenhead she topped up with fuel oil for her coal-burning days were long past. The vessel took on board fresh water, provisions and stores and signed on four more crew members – a greaser, a steward and an able seaman. A young third officer took the place of an elderly third mate who only did coasting.

A weak winter's sun lit up the red-brown rust on her plating as the 'Orford' breasted the long swell of the North Atlantic Ocean. She dug into the heavy sea and pitched the spray across her rebuilt foc's'le. She could have made ten knots but with a sea running it was only eight. The weather became colder and very still. Ice formed on the rigging and grey-white snow clouds drifted close to the topmast light, threating to descend. The Master had asked for a great circle course and the second mate had spent two nights constructing one. It took the old ship deeper and deeper into unknown northern waters. The captain said it was shorter and cheaper that way – and he had the radar to protect him. On the ninth day into the voyage at a position 280 miles south of Greenland the foc's'le head lookout shouted into the silent freezing night:

"Fire! Fire in the forepeak!" He clanged the anchor bell shrilly. "Fire! Fire! Fire in the forepeak." And he rang. And rang. Within moments the storeroom underneath spouted tongues of flame through the door gratings. The second mate set in action the fire drill. Washdown hoses snaked out from the foredeck hydrants. But stayed flat. Empty. The deck lines were frozen solid. The ship's engines were rung onto 'stand-by'. The second officer ran back up to the bridge dismayed.

"No water, sir. The paint will explode!" The radar screen caught his eye. "Sir ... there's something weird showing up ahead of us. It's big. Three miles ahead!"

Captain Jones looked for himself. "You're right. Stop the engines, Second Mate!"

The telegraph rang down the order to the engine room and an eerie stillness settled on the ship. The vessel made way under her own impetus, silent, into the dense white freezing fog. Exploding paint drums blasted out from the stores and with each explosion a tongue of flame leapt high into the white fog like an incandescent ribbon of blinding light.

"Sound abandon ship, Second Mate. Prepare the main lifeboat to embarkation level."

Captain Jones considered themselves to be doomed. A foredeck inferno surrounded by five hatches packed with ammunition. The whole ship would go up like Krakatoa. The entire crew assembled by the lifeboat lowered to the level of the boat deck gunwale. The ship's master inspected them. Counted them. Twenty five.

"All present, Mr Mate?"

"All present, sir."

Some of the seamen were terrified, ragged in haphazard clothes, trembling with fright and by the intense cold. Half dressed and barely awake. The captain addressed them.

"If we stay here much longer we'll all be blown to cosmic dust. And if you get into the lifeboat like that you'll die of exposure almost as quickly. We'll leave in three minutes. Every man to get into thick jumpers, socks and seaboots ... bring blankets and overcoats. Off you go. And sharp about it!"

The men scattered. When they came back the terror had gone; never a more motley crew set themselves to survive the ice-fields of the North Atlantic. The incessant explosions from forward and the sheets of yellow-orange fire lit up the swirling ice-fog like an English bonfire night.

The lifeboat's engine spluttered into life and the second mate nosed her out into the heaving calm of the great ocean. When about a hundred yards from the ship the fog suddenly lifted. A deep sigh broke out from the sailors. Within feet of the ship's bow was an iceberg of such size and enormity had they not seen it with their own eyes they would never have believed it. The forward motion still on the ship was carrying it into a huge arched recess in the iceberg's face. As they gazed dumbfounded the cavernous, vaulted ice-chamber enveloped the ship. Slowly yard by yard, fathom on fathom, hatch upon hatch, the 'Orford' disappeared, crackling and spitting fire into the walls and dome of the iceberg. In five minutes she was gone.

"Well! What do you make of that, Mr Mate?" The lifeboat wallowed in the swell, engines quiet in neutral. The chief officer shook his head in disbelief.

"Unbelievable! Where is she?"

"Inside the iceberg." They edged nearer. The lifeboat became chilled and becalmed. A huge overhang of ice towered above them for a thousand feet. "What do you think, Second Mate?"

"Too cold in there for combustion, sir. She'll be frozen solid in a few hours."

"Chief?"

The chief engineer was speechless at the disappearance of the blazing ship into the depths of the iceberg. Only the third officer, a boy of a man, was excited.

"Let's get her out, sir. In a couple of hours it'll be too late."

"Yes, I believe you're right. Follow her in, Second Mate."

The little craft surged forward towards the ice tunnel. As they entered the iceberg the boat's engine echoed back to them from the depths of the cavern. The light, radiant at the vast spread-arch of the entrance became softer, a blue-green as they moved in deeper. The temperature plummeted. The crew gazed about them with wonder and awe. The vertical ice-walls rose hundreds of feet to a natural dome, vaster and wider than anything built by man. The strength of the ice supporting millions of tons was the strength of finest steel, the tough-brittleness of armoured glass.

The 'Orford' had come to rest in the channel. She was festooned in ice-webs spun around the mast and rigging as if set there by a myriad of ice-spiders. The lifeboat drew up alongside the dangling block-hooks that had been unshipped when they cast off. One by one each man scrambled up the adjacent pilot ladder back on board – numb, dumb and stunned.

"Let me know when you're ready, Chief."

Captain Jones went up onto the bridge with his chief officer and second mate, the third officer and some of the deck crew winched back up the lifeboat when the generator came on. Within five minutes the ship was alive. Lights on. The engines becoming stone cold did not fire at first. Then burst into life.

"Dead slow astern, Second Mate."

The old tramp steamer inched her way out of the iceberg amid a roar of echoes – deafening. They made the open sea and set a new course south. Away from the ice. Then resumed their voyage to St John. It took a week to clear out the debris from the blaze and devastation in the forepeak store. The heat buckled and charred No 1 Hatch bulkhead remained as a relic of the disastrous fire. Only a three foot gap between it and the ammunition boxes had stopped a monumental explosion. The carpenters at Woolwich arsenal had set the gap, not for fire but because of heavy vibrations in a head on gale and the risk of friction heat.

In the event the Yokohama yard did not break her up but sold her to the Shanghai and Inland Sea Shipping Company. Five crew members were repatriated. The rest, including Captain Jones stayed with her. A ship layered in blessings – that some might call lucky. And the ship's company had a deep bond. They were survivors. Furthermore, they loved the old ship.

*

✤ 12 ✤

Miss Hall

Some of you may know the Gasthaus Fruhling but it's unlikely you will have stayed there. Frau Grubel doesn't take in tourists, she finds them too sudden ... suddenly there, suddenly gone. Or strangers, they make her nervous ... she only takes long term residents, and those by recommendation.

None ever said who had recommended Herr Weiss, and there was a mystery about when he had arrived, but he was already there for many years before Miss Hall came. Miss Hall had come from the Franz Josef in the Oberklang Strasse not long after the sudden death of her brother – a pillar of the second violins but who had collapsed during Mahler Three. She then had to move down-market, not having anymore the allowance her brother gave her, as well as paying her hotel bills. Apart from a small allowance that didn't cover the funeral costs that was the last she heard from them. Of course she did hear them at concerts for like her brother she was musical.

Miss Hall was always at breakfast with Herr Weiss though at separate tables at the opposite ends of the room. He always addressed her kindly, almost with a tone of affection. His English was excellent, only the trace of an accent – the voice of a well-educated man. Someone, Miss Hall considered when alone, any woman would be pleased to be with, and at ease.

"Good morning, Miss Hall ... what a nice morning. How well you look today, positively spring-like. A day for Schonbrunn perhaps?"

The faintest flush spread up into Miss Hall's cheeks. She was sure she was not in love with him, not at her age – but she did feel she would have liked at the moment to have stretched out her hand and touched his arm.

"Good morning, Herr Weiss ... thank you. No ... I'm planning to visit the Schubert Museum."

"Ah ... Schubert. Of course, music is your first love. One day I shall ask you to take me to the concert hall and explain everything. As you say in England, 'music is the food of love' ... but we pedestrian workers need to be led to it by more sensitive souls." The flush deepened in Miss Hall's cheeks and for an instant she looked down. She knew he meant it, for her to introduce him into the beauty of the classics – and she was sensitive, her mother had always said so. He added, "It is my work you know, Miss Hall ... I'm kept at it and all the worthwhile things in life pass me by."

But on that morning, perhaps it was the summer's day arriving in such brightness, the leaving behind of a cold spring, she was emboldened.

"Perhaps you'd like to meet me at the café by the museum, Herr Weiss, for some coffee? And if you could spare the time I could show you some of the best exhibits."

"My dear Miss Hall, I would be enchanted. I won't say yes and I won't say no.

It all depends if I can get away. What time would you suggest ... convenient to yourself, of course."

"Should we say two o'clock?"

She waited for him ... and waited – nervously at first clasping her hands and then releasing them, then with a sinking heart as the clock ticked on. He did not come. With some of the brightness gone out of the day she went in to the 3 pm concert *Winterreise*. As the music enfolded her she understood – with a man like Herr Weiss work came first, a man committed to his profession and serving others. For him a little lunchtime relaxation had to go. She knew she was not in love with him but during the sadder moment in the music she shed some tears. *Einsamkeit*. Schubert had touched her heart, in the same way that Herr Weiss must be feeling when he said that the more important moments of life were passing him by.

In the evening when she returned to her room Miss Hall looked at herself in the mirror … not bad looking, her bust a bit small, but people often said that her eyes and her hair were a feature. And yes, her outfit was light, spring-like with a touch of summer just as he had noticed.

The moment he entered the dining room he came straight to her. "Ah, my dear Miss Hall. "He lifted her hand and kissed it." I beg you to forgive me. I was thinking of you constantly, enraged that my work was pinning me down when I should have been there with you, at your side."

Miss Hall fought back tears – such a tender apology. She did forgive him.

"Perhaps there will be another time, Herr Weiss. It is unfair, that I have so much more free time than you. Please don't work so hard that those worthwhile things you mentioned will always pass you by."

"And a worthwhile moment is now, Miss Hall. I would like to take you out this evening to my favourite coffee house."

"Really? Now? I'm not sure if I have the right evening-wear to come out with you, Herr Weiss."

"Nonsense … you are most attractive as you are. This is Vienna … we do not have the buttoned-up shirt."

To her astonishment, once outside he took her arm. A man at ease with women and the world. They walked to a nearby coffee house in the Wilhelmstrasse not far from the casino. So many people smiled and nodded towards Herr Weiss and said *'Guten Abend'* that she felt flattered being with such an important man, a man so well-known and respected.

Gasthaus Fruhling was run smoothly and well by Frau Grubel, a widow. To Miss Hall she frequently seemed unusually warm with Herr Weiss, sometimes teasing and laughing with him. But she was relieved to observe that he always responded in a dignified way as a professional man would, never taking offence. The day that altered Miss Hall's life finally and forever came on a Monday morning towards the end of May. She never liked Mondays. Somehow the day made her feel lonely and unwanted. It was an evening she didn't go out, dining at home. Other days she was out – the English Arts Club where her talents were guided by the kind and gifted Mrs Ackroyd. Thursdays she went to her marimba lessons, Fridays Esperanto, Saturdays the late service at St Stephan's

Cathedral and Sundays, earlier. A special day when she attended and received communion with friends at the English Church.

On that life-changing Monday evening Herr Weiss was unusually absent from his table. Moreover the other two regular diners Professor Stadler and his wife had left that morning for Baden Baden. She was alone. She jumped – a loud rapping on the front door, a jangling of the bell, angry loud voices and suddenly Herr Weiss was marched into the dining room. How very foreign she thought. Such manners and noise – it could never have happened in England, and certainly not in Sidmouth.

On either side of her friend, gripping his arms in an uncouth way, were two large men, pursued by Frau Grubel wide-eyed, pale and dismayed. She remonstrated angrily. "What an effrontery. Disgraceful ... marching into my dining-room and such roughness with my guest. It is outrageous. Release him at once!"

The two grim-faced men, with a distant-eyed Herr Weiss, jerked him to a standstill in front of Miss Hall. She was astonished. Extraordinary ...

"Are you Frau Hall?" One of the men thrust a small oblong piece of paper towards her.

"I am Miss Hall," she answered sharply. Coldly

"We are from the Casino. We did not believe you would have written such a large IOU for this man. This is not the first time, Madame. "

"I am not a Madame, I am Miss Hall. Pass it to me, and take your hands down."

She glanced at Herr Weiss. His face was sphinx-like, pale. She read the credit note and tore it up. "Of course it is mine. I have signed it haven't I?" She reached down to her handbag and wrote a cheque. "You own my friend a deep apology. Take this to your director. I shall write to him in the morning about this gross maltreatment of Herr Weiss and your bursting in here like two uncouth hooligans. Now be off with you, and never show your faces in here again!"

The casino bailiffs hurried out, stung by her icy reprimand. Frau Grubel gave Herr Weiss a long hard look and left them to attend to her sinking strudel. Herr Weiss rubbed his forehead and looked towards Miss Hall for the first time.

"I am sorry that it came to this. I was winning. It should not have happened."

"My poor dear Herr Weiss. Those men were quite beastly. What a dreadful shock you have had. Please bring your knife and fork to my table, Frau Grubel was just about to bring in the goulash. I don't think you should have the cream. One has to be careful. But I don't mind if you order half a carafe of wine. I think white will be best ... and we have *apfelstrudel* to follow".

*

13

The Ming Vase

When Mrs Rillie resigned her teaching post at the age of thirty seven it was not because the new head didn't like her or that she was finding the children harder to cope with – none of these. She had seen a small cottage, one she had always wanted, and decided she must grasp the moment, buy it and bring up her father to share it. He needed looking after though he would deny it hotly, being a fiercely independent spirit.

Two cottages were for sale, side by side. She couldn't afford the larger one but thought hers had its own charm, and a special garden. They were in a coastal village, noted for its oysters, lighthouse and a thatched public house. In the event he came willingly, perhaps he was aware of an unsettling loneliness and increasing deafness. The vase had been in the house on moving in, perhaps overlooked or unwanted by the previous owner. She placed it in the window where the setting sun's light would display its delicate patterns and colours.

Several weeks later when some order and tranquillity had been restored, a man knocked on her door. He had seen the vase in the window.

"Yes?" Mrs Rillie was surprised to be confronted by a stranger. He had a pleasing face and manner.

"I'm really sorry to disturb you ... but I was walking by and couldn't help noticing your vase. It's very attractive. I like ceramics and porcelain."

She invited him in. They talked a little about the vase – and how she had moved it out of the shadows into the light. He told her about London and how he was down for the weekend – how he was taken with her village and its lighthouse. She made tea and placed an assortment of biscuits on a plate that had been a favourite with her mother. As he was leaving he hesitated.

"I suppose you're not thinking of selling that vase ... it is quite unusual ... would you allow me to offer fifty pounds for it?" He shrugged and then smiled. "Sorry ... rather a cheek."

She sold it – because there was something about him she admired. After supper she told her father how a Mr Sargent had called, a really nice man, and she'd sold him her Chinese vase. For fifty pounds. His eyes widened. He removed his glasses. His hearing aid began to whistle. He tapped it.

"Was that wise, dear? It's Ming. Chenghua, 1485."

"I know."

"Then why did you do it? I don't understand."

"He wanted it so much."

"Margaret. It is worth a great deal of money."

But she only smiled, went to the mirror and touched her hair.

Mr Sargent was so excited with his purchase he scarcely noticed the journey back to London. At the next sale in his auction house he slipped in his new acquisition, placing upon it a reserve price of twenty thousand pounds. In the event a telephone bidder and an Edinburgh museum battled it out, the price spiralling up to more than twice the reserve. The sale was made. £59,750.

But a week later Mr Sargent was struck down by an overwhelming and consuming guilt. It began insidiously. He began to wake at 3 am in a cold sweat and heavy quick heartbeat. No sleep returned – he watched the day break, heard the dawn chorus and the milk float coming down the road. In his mind's eye was an image of Mrs Rillie, and echoing in his head disturbing thoughts about her elderly father. After a further week when his appetite went he consulted a friend, a retired doctor. He was advised to have a break from work, take a holiday in Italy – the sun, the art, the complete change of scene. He went out with a group but left them after five days, nothing he saw entered the greyness of his heart. He then applied for sick leave which was granted with much sympathy – he was well liked and a respected specialist who never took holidays or time off.

Sleep evaded him totally. His eyes became heavy and dull and the depression spread from his mind to all parts of the body. A week later he took himself to the Hungerford Bridge. Mr Sargent paced up and down it all night, gazing first at the miraculous lights of the great unsleeping city, the illuminated dome of St Paul's, the square shapes on the South Bank, but his eyes were finally drawn down to the dark tumbling waters. He watched the ebb tide, the slack water and waited for the flood to come back towards him.

"All right, sir?"

At 4 am, a policeman moved him off the bridge and walked him to the kiosk used by all-night taxi drivers. The officer bought two cups of coffee. They sat on a bench in Victoria Embankment Gardens and he asked the distraught man what it was all about. Mr Sargent told him the whole story, how he had bought a vase he had known to be Ming and highly valuable from an unsuspecting widow for a pittance. Ever since he had been overwhelmed by guilt – and bitterly regretted his moment of greed and folly.

"'Tis better that you pay it all back, sir. Nothing is worth all this doom and gloom."

Mr Sargent sold his mansion flat and resigned from the auction house. He bought the larger cottage next to Mrs Rillie. When he had settled in, he put a proposition to her.

"Mrs Rillie, as you know I have come down here for my health. I'm sorry to have shocked you once again, and that now you have to put up with me as your immediate neighbour."

"My dear Mr Sargent," Mrs Rillie flushed and touched his arm, "my father and I couldn't be more pleased."

Mr Sargent sighed with relief and relaxed. "You will excuse me for observing that your own house is considerable smaller than mine, and you have your elderly father living with you as well." She was looking at him, into his eyes. "I propose to open a small antiques shop here. Right here."

She smiled from the heart. "Really ... but how thrilling!"

"Unfortunately I shall need more space." He paused. A sense of humour appeared to invade his eyes. "What I am about to suggest may surprise you." He laughed lightly and waved a finger in a donnish manner. "I propose that we knock our two houses into one, build a neat and comfortable extension for your father and by way of compensation for all that rude shock and upheaval I will make you an award of £59,750 pounds together with a partnership in our shop."

Mrs Rillie was stunned. After a few minutes, still shaking but inwardly smiling, she left Mr Sargent's house and returned to her own. She put a new battery into her father's hearing aid and explained all that had happened next door.

"Did you say £59,750 pounds? My goodness!"

"Yes, father."

"Of course ... that would be the value of your Ming vase."

"I know."

Mr Sargent's offer was accepted. The building work was carried out promptly and with care – the builder had been affected by the economic downturn and had no orders. The contract saved him from winding up his business and having to go to work on Felixstowe Docks. Moreover he took on a carpenter and bricklayer from the village, taking both men off Job Seeker's allowance and restoring harmony into both families. When the work was done, the builder's contract was extended to provide a discreet car park with landscaping to a design by Mrs Rillie herself. They engaged a full-time gardener – odd jobs man.

The shop was an immediate success. Mr Sargent had an international reputation and was considered sound in many fields, not only porcelain. In high summer a marquee was erected in the car park and Mrs Rillie's father displayed pieces of porcelain from Penang. At the end of the third year Mr Sargent proposed to Mrs Rillie and was accepted. On her wedding night Mr Sargent returned to Mrs Rillie the Ming vase which he had been able to buy back. He spoke to her severely.

"Margaret, you should never have parted with this beautiful vase in such a careless manner. I cannot think what got into you. The whole matter caused me great distress. If only you had consulted with your father first ..."

The smile she gave him was not about a Ming vase. At that moment their bodies were touching and her thoughts were elsewhere.

*

❈ 14 ❈

He was unexpected

The English like Dinard – its wide sandy beaches, and dogs may be hired for walking along the promenade. Very sensibly the town council set aside squares of coarse grass with a sign of the squatting dog and a notice

'Attention! – pour les chiens seulement.'

In recent years the English had stayed away. The whole town was affected. None more so than 'Pension Russe'. It was too far from everywhere, the airport and the town, too far for the German joggers and too close for the Swedish 10,000 metre runners who trained there, and too far from the beach. Imagine the joy of Madame Honfleur when an elderly woman arrived in May, upon an old bicycle wearing a wide-brimmed sunhat, with a small white case on her back pannier and a large handbag in the front basket. The *patronne* came out.

"Yes, Madame?"

"I require some rooms." Her French was foreign.

"Some rooms, Madame? ... then please come in."

"I have tried other places – very tiresome, quite unsuitable. The rooms are no bigger than my cupboards. There isn't a tap to be seen."

"This house is overflowing with taps, Madame."

"Good. I never drink water, but I wash in it. Why are you called *'Pension Russe'*?"

"My mother, Madame, had a Russian vine at the back. It's not there anymore. My husband ... he is very difficult ... he poisoned it. My mother died soon after that cruelty ... Dr Laportier said it was the shock. My neighbour said some of the weed-killer entered her water supply. But she is malicious. We were all unaffected."

"Where is your husband."

"The casino, Madame. He is always there. May I take you upstairs?"

"Are these rooms linked by doors?"

"Only from the passage, Madame. This is a respectable house. We are Catholics."

They went upstairs. "I see. I shall have to have some building work done."

"Building work, Madame?"

"Yes. What is your name?"

"Madame Honfleur."

"I shall need glass doors between these rooms. I shall take them all. You may have two years rent in advance. I am Princess Alexandrina. But when my English friends come you may call me Alice. The English cannot manage names longer than six letters. I am not a corridor person. I need space and air."

Madame Honfleur flushed. She had always regretted the infamous revolution. She flexed her knee. "I am sure my cousin can put in some doors for you, Princess."

They were pleasing rooms, large windows to the west with the afternoon sun and a view of the sea. The back windows looked out over potato fields already in white flower, and beyond tall green spikes of new sweet-corn.

The new doors were carefully fitted, chosen by the two women together from designs shown to them by the manager of a glass works. They selected an embossed glass of a floral pattern, leaf swirls and a trace of amber in the buds. Both were enchanted with the result. The husband was indifferent. He no longer loved his wife. Madame Honfleur was delighted with her new guest and quickly felt an affection for her, a ray of warmth in her loveless life. She called her Alice or 'Princess', but the older woman only ever addressed her as 'Madame Honfleur'. They exchanged embroidery patterns and went for long walks with the dog 'Victor Hugo' – a Welsh corgi, left behind by an Edinburgh lady who said its breathing was too heavy and distasteful. On Saturday evenings when

Monsieur Honfleur stayed all night in the casino, Madame Honfleur would go upstairs, sit with her friend and they would listen to music together.

On a cool day in November with a raw wind coming off the sea, a young man approached the guest house from the bus stop. He had a spring in his stride. His head was shaven and in both ears he wore studs and earrings – on each shoulder tattoos. He knocked firmly on the door.

Madame Honfleur was startled. The man addressed her in faultless French.

"I wish to see my grandmother."

"Your grandmother?"

"The Princess Alexandrina Nestorova."

"She is out walking with Victor Hugo and won't be back for some time."

But the clear, firm voice of her friend reached her from the kitchen and a breathless Welsh corgi came running in. It growled at the young man. Close behind, lead loose in her left hand followed Princess Alexandrina.

She stared, dismayed at the sight of her grandson.

"What are you doing here, Viktor?"

"I need a cheque, Grandmaman."

"You have startled us. Now introduce yourself to my dear friend here, Madame Honfleur."

He bowed to the younger woman. "Count Viktor Nestorov, Madame."

The Princess shook her head in annoyance. "He only finds me when he wants money."

Her friend touched her arm. "Monsieur Honfleur is the same, Princess. He only has the allowance I provide."

"Quite so. Very wise." She turned to the young man. "What is it this time, Viktor?"

"Some paintings are coming up for auction at Sotheby's, Grandmaman. They are by Ilya Repin, and we should take them back to our house in Lyskovo." He showed her the catalogue. "They belong in Russia."

The older lady sighed, went to her desk and wrote a cheque for a considerable sum. The man's face fell when he saw it.

"But it is made out to the Auction House, Grandmaman."

"Don't come back here, Viktor. We are not receiving visitors, especially from my family."

Her grandson flushed, shrugged, placed the cheque in his wallet and left without another word. The door closed and the house became silent once more. Madame Honfleur was already downstairs in the kitchen. Her friend reached for her hand. "Come along, my dear, leave all that. It has stopped raining. Now we can take Viktor Hugo for his walk."

They walked arm-in-arm along the empty promenade. The warmth from their arms passed from one to the other. The wind was cold, cutting and from the east. It may have been ice in the wind that brought tears into the eyes of both women. Or the coldness of the world.

*

✣ 15 ✣

Lizard

He slept mostly in the open. When it rained he would try and find any shelter there was – a hollow tree, a barn, a cowshed, an uprooted oak. He travelled with a small backpack in which he kept a sewing kit, spare socks and shirt, a bottle for water, a towel and a small bar of soap. Lately he had acquired an umbrella. It needed stitches. Which he put in. It folded. He liked that. On a sandy warm outcrop he had also given a home to a companion.

As the years passed the walker, Victor, became more and more shut in, encapsulated. He had found ways of avoiding contemptuous stares – anxious looks from women, taunts and mockery of children. Dogs. Some were persistent, snapping and growling – for those he had a pungent aerosol – others just came up out of curiosity, and compassion. A few licked his hand and travelled with him until they disappeared.

Yet in all his solitude and endless walking he was not alone. In the pocket of his coat lived the sand lizard. George. It had found its way in there on a hot summer's day needing shade. When Victor lay down to rest George watched over him, crouching in the manner of an alert guardian upon his master's shoulder, using its long tongue to fend off flies that circled his head.

On the 18 of April, as the wet and chill of winter was leaving the land, upon an unmade road that once had felt the pounding feet of a Roman legion, Victor suddenly fell ill. He was overwhelmed by shaking and a high fever. The rattling of his bones was as if his mother had risen from the dead and was shaking him like a rat in a fury. Then shut him in the cupboard. The punishment for wetting. Something he did … often.

The heat burning him up subsided into shivering and flashing lights. He fell and fainted.

By chance, fate or a blessing, there came from behind him another walker. Ernest lived alone in a railway cottage, a seasoned rambler, firm boots, a staff, ordinance survey map, compass and a waterproof cap. As he drew close to the rags in the centre of the old track, he discovered a wreck of a person. From beneath the man's check shirt poked out the head of a lizard.

"Good Heavens!" Ernest started back, "What's all this? What do we have here?"

He was a kindly man with the nature of a Samaritan, a man who had been a carer all his life in a care-home. A strong man much loved. He buttoned the raincoat around the slumped figure singing softly as he did so, thinking the song would calm the lizard as a flute might for a snake. Ernest lifted the man astonished at his lightness. The tramp inside the fawn raincoat weighing no more than a child. He carried the unconscious man to an ancient building that straddled the Roman road – as a fort or gatehouse might have done in the centuries of occupation. Rain had begun to fall quickly and he hurried inside. In the crumbling building he tried to find a resting place for the sick man, not the first derelict he had gathered in.

The rooms he entered were dark, damp and mildewed. The passing winter had been long and wet. All except one strange room – a very curious place that made him feel uneasy ... disbelieving. Along a wall was a raised marble bench, the stone cold to his touch – but not wet, no condensation ... dry. On the walls were faded drapes of scarlet and gold linen, yet it seemed that a single touch would thrust them to the floor in a cloud of powder. There was an aroma in the room, the smell of herbs, camphor or the suggestion of incense. He laid the vagrant gently down onto the bench and took from his own pack a towel, slipping it under the head of the unconscious man.

"You'll be all right here, my friend, for a while. I'll try and find you some help. But it won't be that easy way out here on a Sunday afternoon."

Ernest left him, troubled ... he would phone in from the next house or call box.

The lizard George came out from an inner pocket, crouched and kept guard though there were no flies, no bats, only a soft rain-breeze entering through the open door that brushed the fabrics releasing their perfume.

In the night when a large harvest moon shone through a gap in the roof Victor woke up.

He knew at once it was the big cupboard he had been trying to escape from all his life. A room with the smells he was so familiar. With the darkness he was so familiar. But he was not locked in. The moon was shining, filling the space he was in with light. He sat up. The fever had gone. He had no idea how he had entered this place, where it was, who had brought him here – but this time his entry to it was different, quite different, without the shaking, slapping and screams. He believed now, in this waking moment, he had been placed there by an angel. Victor stood up. The moment of standing momentarily made him dizzy, but it passed. A water-bottle had been left beside him. He unscrewed it and drank deeply. A guardian angel or Samaritan had passed that way, blessed and cared for him.

He spoke to the crouching figure of George. "George, something rare has happened. We have been visited by an angel and he has taken that old cupboard with him. We can leave here now. That old nightmare has been breathed on and turned to dust. The pain has been lifted from my head. We have been blessed. Let us go home now."

Outside the rain had stopped. The southerly breeze was ushering in a warmth as a new dawn was breaking. Victor walked forward in firm strides, as if his childhood terrors had been swept away. The light of day on him was a new light. Bright and uplifting.

*

❈ 16 ❈

Miss Whitby

"Goodbye, Doris."

Miss Whitby watched her friend leave and pressed the stopwatch in her pocket. She closed the door, moving her trainers into the shoe recess.

In the kitchen on a shelf were her notebooks. Taking the watch from her pocket she laid it carefully on the table, lifted down a leather-bound diary marked 'Visitors', turned to 'D' and smoothed down the page. Beneath the entry for Doris were two sets of figures.

Miss Whitby took the diary pen and in the first column headed 'LV' – length of visit – she marked in carefully: 45mins 42 secs. She smiled and allowed her eyes to rise up from the page. Doris had stayed for 45 minutes seven times before – and seven was her special number. Not a holy number, the vicar disapproved of such things and had quite roughly told her so.

After entering Doris's visit, she turned to her calculator and brought up the average time for visits over the last three years. 23 mins,17 seconds. It was very pleasing – clearly Doris was now staying with her much longer, their friendship was deepening – and since last year Aug. 19 11.17 am, she always came with a cake.

She said aloud in the direction of James, the budgie, "Our friendship is becoming quite special. Doris is coming out of herself since Albert died." Turning back to the day's entry she noted in the 'Comments' column ... 'very talkative today and Dundee.' Dundee cake was her meaning, not news about her niece who didn't live in that part of Scotland.

Transferring the stop-watch – once her father's – to the pocket in her track-suit, she was ready to go out for the training run. Ten miles –

a toning up for the forthcoming Ladies Marathon. The day was bright with a keen east wind off the sea – good for running, stinging the face and opening the lungs. The road left the town and began a long incline up an escarpment. She then turned off the hill onto an unmarked road that led to the Common. Click went her stop-watch after the first mile – always the slowest because of the uphill climb out of the village. Miss Whitby ran each mile in ten minutes, which gave her an overall time for the 26 miles of 4 hours 24. Slower than when she had been national cross-country champion – but now she was older. Sixty. It was not sensible or practical to run under 4 hours anymore.

She had nearly not entered the marathon. A list of grievances – firstly the committee said she was too old and then that her membership of the harriers had lapsed. Thirdly, she was disliked by Wendy Fullblow.

The day of the race began badly. She could not find her stop-watch. Miss Whitby was badly shaken. It was a treasure, always travelled with her – and now it was gone. She lined up with the ladies feeling as lost as if she'd lost a spiked shoe in the 5,000 metres. Wendy Fullblow came to her.

"You must be Miss Whitby. I have been hearing about you."

Miss Whitby shuddered. She avoided her eyes and looked out across the woman's shoulder. There encouraging and smiling was Doris, and she was waving a Union Jack. The starting official had his flag raised. She hurried up to him.

"Mr Hardbrake, I wondered if I might borrow a watch, please."

"A watch, Miss Whitby? But surely you have one of your father's stop-watches."

"I have mislaid it. I was thinking so much about today I put it down somewhere, and now it's lost." Her voice trembled. Her eyes became moist.

"Dear me, how unfortunate. I couldn't possibly let you have this one, it's the gold watch from my firm. It's too old and precious to be jerked about in such a long race. Sorry."

She was so disappointed. The women were ready to go. Some had come up to the line, toes against it, leaning forward in a starting pose anxious to be off. Miss Whitby walked away from them to Doris. "Doris, could I borrow your watch. I can't find mine."

"Oh dear. Poor you. What bad luck!" She un-strapped the watch from her wrist. "Take it with pleasure, Eleanor. But it can stop, anytime, anywhere. It needs cleaning." Miss Whitby took it, sighed and pushed it down into her pocket, the space when her own watch always sat and comforted her.

"Thanks. You are so good, Doris." She touched her cheek and hurried away. Mr Hardbrake had the flag poised and was looking crossly in her direction. He brought it down when she was still quite a way from them, then shrugged and turned away.

She was with the pack after a few minutes, after all her training was always uphill for the first mile and here it was level. After the first mile they were all still bunched together. Miss Whitby felt for Doris's watch and lifted it out. Stopped. Her heart quickened. "Oh dear. I shall have to stay with them now." She moved up closer to the front runners. Wendy Fullblow and three younger athletes stared at her. That annoyed her and Miss Whitby kicked on to the front. Was she not once the national champion, not some old pensioner to be examined as a freak. And she was running on air. It was one of those days, light feet – floating over the ground.

At the ten mile drinks station she was still ahead. Miss Whitby slowed and grasped the offered water, which she drank quickly and threw away. Then she took a plastic cup of Lucozade from the man on the advertising stall. "Well done," he said. "You're showing them." She glanced over her shoulder.

Wendy Fullblow was not in sight. She realised then that she had no need of her stop watch, her body was locked into the old rhythm, unchangeable and relentless – 10 miles in the hour, 4hrs 24 for the race. She then relaxed, acknowledged the clapping of the spectators, smiled and quickened her stride. Not because she needed to but today was a golden day, running was effortless and a pleasure. She began to sing as a happiness invaded her. She had not run in this way since Belgium – a long time ago. In some strange way she hoped the race would never end – she was running into a spiritual world that her father used to talk about when at a certain moment in racing a door chinks open and the mind begins to travel ahead of the body in grace and vision. Strange and deep things that some may hear about and a few, once or twice in their lives, may enter.

The finish line, the tape and Mr Hardbrake's Morris Minor came closer. She could run on past everyone on to the sea, down the beach into the waves. And she was waving. The breaking of surf on a beach was like a voice cheering and calling her.

But once through the tape she did stop. She was neither tired nor breathless, simply elated – and so very happy.

"I say, Miss Whitby, what an astonishing run. Quite amazing! You have broken the women's record. Do you know you've clocked a time of 3 hours 36. Quite astonishing These are times from when you ran for England!"

Miss Whitby was followed in by a Kenyan student from the polytechnic. Third was a Chinese violinist from the Conservatoire. Wendy Fullblow was last.

In bed that night Miss Whitby had two dreams. In the first she dreamed she was a guest on 'A question of sport'. The presenter was asking her if she had heard of Wendy Fullblow. Her reply was gracious.

"I do know her, of course. Quite a good marathon runner. A prospect for the future, but lacking at present in experience." A kindly comment she thought. In the second dream she saw the Angel of the Lord appear, within the moonlight of her room. He held in his arms a huge stop-watch.

"What is that?" she asked.

"It is the stop-watch of your life, Eleanor Whitby."

"Really. How long will it run for, before it stops?"

"Eighty-nine years, nine months, three days, five hours, thirty three minutes and seventeen seconds." The angel smiled at her reassuringly.

"Oh, good." She smiled back shyly and fell into a deep sleep.

Next morning she found the watch in a pocket in her old three A's track suit which she had tried on to look at herself in the mirror. Doris came round to ask for her watch back. To Miss Whitby's surprise it was working again.

"You ran like the wind, Eleanor. And you seemed in a sort of heaven."

"Yes. It was a bit like that."

Doris stayed for one hundred and four minutes, ten seconds. That was because Miss Whitby asked her to come on holiday with her. Not running – just long walks.

*

✣ 17 ✣

Wolf Tree

"The boy has arrived, Professor Lavalle. Your student ... David Wolff."

But I was not quite ready. The name ... and a memory. "Thank you. Ask him to wait a minute, please."

The memory. In those days we were three – Grandmaman Emilie, Jacques – our gardener and odd job man who lived in the garden house but joined us for supper – and myself, a boy of ten, over-sensitive, nervous and full of fears. My parents had been interned by the Paris Gestapo. They were betrayed. And taken to a death camp. I mourn their deaths to this day, and for ever. What I'm about to describe took place in the grey cold post-war years.

I had a friend in class at school whose name was Paul Dessin. One memorable day we were taken by his father, a teacher at the Lycée Clemenceau, to see a nature film. I was overjoyed and thrilled with my first cinema. So many children were there, such a buzz of excitement. That film changed me. I was transfixed by images of a small white elephant. My friend's father explained that any creature could be white, even wolves, even children from Africa.

The following night I had the dream for the first time. The tree outside my bedroom window – a dying conifer – had half way up it a white wolf staring at me. I woke up with a shriek, my throat dry and crept out of bed to reassure myself. The moon was behind the tree – thin and new. No wolf. My heart slowed but before getting back into bed I opened my door wide to let in the landing light. I pulled the blankets over my head and hugged my Bruno, the only toy rescued from our old home.

A bad dream. I thought no more about it. Not till five weeks later. Suddenly the exact same dream, only this time there were two white wolves in the tree. I must have screamed for Jacques. He was downstairs with grandmaman and came hurrying up. He held my hand until I calmed down.

"Jacques, there are two wolves watching me." Grandmaman came up and stood beside him.

"Where, *mon petit*?"

"In the tree outside." My tears came back. She held me in her arms then went to my window.

"Not any more, Chéri … only the moon. Your shouts must have frightened them away." She stayed with me in the armchair until I fell asleep.

Nothing happened for a year. Then they came back. Three this time, and so horrible. All with their teeth bared. I was convinced they were about to jump down, come for me and eat me up. I screamed and screamed. Grandmaman Emilie took me into her bed and there I sobbed myself to sleep. For days I was in a state of terror – white wolves with yellow eyes, so terrifying. I couldn't sleep in my room and Nana put up a camp bed beside hers. I knew those creatures were out there looking for me.

I started my new school that week and things faded. A year passed. I was good at school. M. Dessin, Paul's father, praised my work and all seemed well. And I was a good runner. I found distance running easy and the school had an athletics track … the Lycée was famous for it. I was the best in the junior school. What a day that was when I won the 3,000 metres and was presented at the end of year assembly with a track suit and running shoes with spikes.

Yet that night my worst ever terror returned. I thought I should die. In the dream tree were four white wolves slobbering and licking their jaws as if they could taste my flesh already. My screams must have been terrifying to hear. Jacques rushed in from his garden house. Emilie held me in her arms all night I was told – because I had fainted. They sent for Dr Laportier who gave me a spoon of a strange syrup and I knew no more till morning. By the end of the week the dying pine tree was cut down to the ground and the wood burned – not on our woodstove, but in a huge bonfire.

A following morning I came downstairs late. The doctor's syrup made me heavy and drowsy. I was finding it hard to get up. Grandmaman was outside the kitchen door. I could hear her talking to Jacques. Not about the tree. She was holding out the morning newspaper and speaking to him in a low voice.

"Jaques ... he is dead. Wolf Carpentier was shot last night. They recovered his body from the Seine."

I heard Jacques spit and grind his foot into the gravel. "*Merde!* The pig. You should have let me kill him first, Madame Eli."

"No. You are my friend as well as my gardener. Not an assassin. Our boys found him at last."

"*Cochon*! The dirty pig should have been strangled. Slowly!"

I crept away upstairs. I knew at once that my dream would never come back ...

Such a memory. I am trembling.

"Show the lad up please, Béatrice."

The little boy entered my rooms grasping his violin. I placed my hand on his shoulder. "What is your name again please, boy."

"David Wolff. Monsieur le Maitre."

"Ah ... so it is. And what have you prepared for me today?"

"I have been practising a little piece by Gustav Mahler, sir."

"Really? But surely you are too young for all his sadnesses? Go on ... let me hear it."

It was an arrangement of a Ruckert song. *Einsamkeit.* Loneliness.

I turned my head away and wept. It was a song my mother sang. I walked out.

Jacques was standing there arranging my mail.

"I can't take this boy, Jacques. Can't you hear what he's playing!"
"But you must, Joseph. The angels have sent him."

*

❈ 18 ❈

Lady with a dog

Dr Liadev was a big man. The sadness that had inserted itself was not that of arrival, or a mood held at bay in the train. Something else. Indefinable. He detached himself from the stream of people heading for buses, turned into a side street and found himself on the Northern Promenade looking out over a river at the restless flow of life along the road on the farther bank.

The doctor took off his overcoat – he had come over too warm and to his annoyance a sweat had broken out across his forehead. He sat down on a bench, conscious of a quickening pulse, aware he no longer had a young heart and smiled at a woman passing in front of him with a white dog.

"Good morning."

She returned his smile. "It's still warm. My dog likes this weather." She bent down to touch the dog's head. "He's spoiled. Come along, Gaga."

"Gaga? He's not a sensible dog?"

"Gagarin." She walked away. Liadev was disappointed, he would have liked to talk some more, ask about her life and how she was coping with all the changes. Several yards on Gaga lingered at a bush. The woman waited, adjusted her hat as if unaware of the man, a large man with an engaging manner. As she called the dog, their eyes met. Liadev raised his hat in her direction, in sympathy and amusement – pleased she smiled back. So unlike Moscow. Her smile warmed him, and saddened, reminding him he had no wife who would smile at him like that. He wondered who she was, why she was not at work … or perhaps on holiday? Absurd questions for which there could never be an answer. He hoped very much that she would turn around to walk back his way.

The doctor opened his briefcase, took out his mother's letter and opened it absently, his thoughts still lingering with the lady and her dog – her image coming from a more certain, more tender past.

GORKY 1.11. 1991. 8a/17 Oktobroskaya.
Dearest Maximoushka,
I hope you will find time and a quiet place to read this. It will be long because I have a lot to tell you and some very special news. First let me say I couldn't ask you first, she didn't arrive until October 16, two weeks after you left me for Moscow. Then Irina – you remember, at 4a – she tried ringing your office. You're lucky to have such a nice girl working for you. Irina says Sasha speaks to her on the telephone just like a daughter. She said you had gone off again, on your travels. What I am saying in my silly roundabout way is that Natalya has come to live with us. Now don't be cross. You know you've always liked her and she thinks the world of you ...'

Dr Liadev became aware of the sun's warmth on his face. He raised his eyes from the letter and watched columns of water-dazzle trace across the river towards him. He looked away, the light too bright, and watched a file of ducks swimming through the slack water. A drake with two females. He read on.

'... of course, you may remember Natalya was married to Martin, the big Swedish man who repaired buses in Central Moscow. You couldn't go to the funeral and Natalya quite understood. They had a Transport Directive flat but she had to move out. Thankfully she found work looking after an old man on his own who needed someone to live in. But one day, he had to go to live with his brother in Leningrad. So she was without a home yet again. Well, a real surprise, Natalya caught a train and there she was, on our doorstep saying, 'Auntie, can you put me up for a bit while I try to get a job, please.'

What could I say – my sister's only daughter. Now whatever you're thinking, it is lovely to have her with me, such a nice kind woman, and company for me in the long winter nights. She wants to do a lot of the cooking but I wasn't having that. Two women in one kitchen? But I have let her cook a few things when I was tired, watching television. I have told her she must be quiet when you come home because you have important government papers to read, and she must keep the TV turned down and not sing or laugh. Natalya has a funny laugh, which might annoy you, and when she laughs it starts me off. She'll sleep in my room when you come home and I have given her two drawers in my bedroom.

Dearest Maximoushka, I do hope you're not cross with me in taking in your cousin. She has found a job at GAZ, the rent money is useful, and I do love her being here, she's like a daughter. I'm sorry this has been such a rambling letter, but I had to explain everything.
With all my tender thoughts, may God always bless and protect you,
Your loving Mama. XXX

ps. Don't wear the thick socks I sent you too soon because you know how your feet easily sweat and it will bring back your athlete's foot.

He left the letter on his knees. It seemed the day was lighter, the sun stronger, and winter was being held at bay. Not annoyed – he felt a deep sense of relief, and of all his cousins, Natalya was his favourite. He was smiling now and did not mind if the lady with the white dog returned home another way. He found himself laughing at no one. The company in front of him was three ducks. They had come up for bread.

*

✥ 19 ✥

You'd better come in, Bobby

I have always known that I've lived before. It is rare, but I'm not the only one.

January 2. I'm at last out. Actually I asked them to keep me in another day. Three years inside is a nasty chunk out of a man's life. I've done some deep thinking this time. In three years you can make a lot of enemies, a few friends – for me neither. I kept to myself and worked outside in the gardens and picking up rubbish. I'm a good gardener. It runs deep into my family – generations. I am different. I was born with a hole in my head. Peggy, my house-mother said it was a bump of knowledge. Mr Anders said it was where all my brains leaked out. Whatever – it hurts sometimes, and not just when it's going to rain.

When I was younger they used to see I was met – prison visitors, trainee probation officers … a curate once. This woman … she's coming over. God help us. Doesn't anyone up there answer a prayer, 'Leave me alone.' She comes right up to me and looks into my eyes. I stare back. She is giving me weird goose-pimples. Whatever profession she's in, it's not probation.

"Go away. I don't need you."

She's not listening. Is she deaf? Still looking into my face. Is it my soul she's after. I lost it to Mr Anders in the children's home. "I hate it when people like you meet me. It's an insult to my space. Why don't you lot do some good work somewhere else? I'm a free man … let me breathe in this free air. Please … go away!"

She's younger than most of them – not pretty. Definitely plain, and those glasses do nothing for her – or that headscarf and chunky pendant. Someone should tell her.

"I haven't come to meet you."

"That's a nice one. Who told you to say that?" I am made coarse by prison. She looks down. I've hurt her. "OK. You're not meeting me. That's a relief. There's no other crushed soul coming out. You've got the wrong day." She is quite young. I can see now beyond the glasses and that charwoman type headscarf. There are tears in her eyes. I have no right to be a bore. Upsetting her. "Who is it you want? I'll give you what I know." The wrong thing to say, I shall be stuck with her now.

"I saw you and came over."

"What d'you mean 'saw me and came over'? You thought I was a celeb? In this crap outfit. I don't do signatures." She is uncomfortable and blushing. I'm being a pain – no manners left. I've slopped them away, so many times. And too much solitary. Of my own choosing. I am ashamed of going back inside. So bloody crass. Well I've been thinking about that. A man can be a moron for only so long. Unless he has rigor mortis of the brain. I told the judge. "I am guilty, Your Honour. A prat and a moron. I apologise to everyone. Believe me – I really am sorry. And for the injury to Mr Anders. Fate put him in front of me in the ABC, in the queue. I simply squeezed his neck so he could feel it, like we did as kids. It was a demonstration, not done with intent to harm. The broken jaw when he fainted was a pure accident, my Lord. Violence, sir, is not part of my nature."

And I was indeed sorry. The man had a brace. The judge was not happy about that. Three years. Setting the balance right. I say to this unhappy woman beside me, "Do I look like someone else. An ex of yours? .... They're mostly all ex's in the nick."

"I know you."

That rocked me. How the hell can she know me, a nobody who no longer writes a diary. That's why she gives me the shivers – a voice from my past. Maybe she was in Ransomes as well. Kids came and went – a few months, a few years. "What's your name ... Alice?" Why in God's name did I say that name?

"Yes. I'm Alice."

"Alice, if you don't mind me saying, you're a weirdo."

"Why did you call me Alice?"

"How do I know. It must be all this free air. It has surged into the hole in my head. Who am I supposed to be?" She is making me uneasy. I have that chill feeling again. Has Moses sent down some avenging angel?

"You're Robert. Everyone called you Bobby. Except me."

"No way! I'm Brian, ever since my unfortunate birth and they dug me out. Maybe my feet were showing. Look, Alice, I'm longing for a decent cup of coffee and one of those fresh croissants. Come with me. There's a place I go to when I come out. I dream of it every night."

"I'm already late for work, Robert. It's my first week back."

"Then be later still. Take a half day. Say your friend advised it." I am smiling at her for the first time. She's so innocent. Pray that she'll stay like that. Are You listening up there – give this one a chance. "So who is this Robert, Alice … your sweetheart. Your loving husband?"

"My husband once."

"Once?"

"Yes."

"Sorry. Don't mind me. I was born with my mouth open and brain closed. Come on then, come with me – take five."

In the café she is still studying me. There is a soft look in her eyes. Is she deranged. Has she just come out of somewhere like me? Now she's slipping her locket and chain off her neck. She clicks it open – a sort of cameo. Enamel. It's old – from her granny? A photo.

"Have a look, Robert."

I did. "Good Lord. I agree, your husband did look like me. Bit older … but I see what you mean. But not me, Alice … no way – I'm a Brian, never a Robert. The uniform? And an officer? That's an old outfit."

"It is you, Robert."

"Yeah. Yeah." I look closer. It's like looking in a mirror. I hate the army, war and all that stupidity. Never again. The guy's bought it. Like so many of those poor devils. I pass it back.

"He seems OK. My better half!"

"I always carry it. And his decoration."

She hasn't finished with me yet. How did I get landed with this woman from another world? She produces a small box from her handbag, opens it and shows me. A military medal.

I read 'Distinguished Service Order and Bar. For extreme gallantry. Western Front 1916. Awarded to Lt. R J Smalley. London Rifles.'

I'm shaking. What the hell do I know about all this. Why am I churned up? Thank God the waiter is here with our coffees and croissants. I feel them. They are soft and warm. He's brought some strawberry jam.

"Thanks. Just right. Are you new here? Where's Jacques?"

He shrugs. He has an accent. It isn't French. "Jacques is at a funeral. I bin here long time. Maybe four years. I'm Tony."

I pass Alice her mug and push the croissants towards her. "Why are you showing me this medal, Alice? It's weird. I don't agree with state violence. It's not my thing."

"But it is your medal."

She's spooking me. "Since when did they think fit to give a low-born, no-hoper like me a commission. And I have no courage. Not like this hero."

"Please keep it, Robert. I've been looking for you for so long."

"Now don't just fly away like a sparrow. Give me your address. I'll look at this and bring it back. It's yours not mine."

She writes it down on the back of the bill: 'Alice Smalley. 64 Cremorna Villas, Fulham SW6', smiles and is gone. All that has really shaken me. One of us is round the twist. I have other things to do. After-care has found me a hotel room in Argyle Square, Kings Cross. I have to check in and report.

It's not till Sunday I get round to taking back Alice's medal. I'm used to Fulham. I went a few times to Craven Cottage, on the trolley-bus. The road's not hard to find. They're all the same – grey brick, two storeys, every terrace identical to the next. I don't say that my heart isn't beating a bit quick. It's about half way down. 62 and then 66. Sixty-four is fresh air – a space for beams ... props against the walls. I knock at sixty-six ... someone is in. A kid answers

"Yes. Can I help you?" I'm amazed. So gracefully said.

"I'm looking for someone ... she said I should come to sixty-four. But ..." I opened my palms to the sky.

"Will you wait a minute please. I'll have to call my grandmother."

A small woman wearing an apron and dark blue stockings comes towards me slowly. She is staring into my face. Just like Alice.

I said, "Sorry. There must be a mistake. Alice told me sixty-four. She left me a valuable medal. A wartime decoration for gallantry. I can't keep it."

"Alice who?"

"Smalley ... lived next door. Nothing there now."

She's giving me the weirdo treatment. Her hand reaches forward. "There is no sixty-four. It went in the blitz. My aunt lived there ... with her husband and baby."

"Oh. But how about Alice and her husband. His medal ... a hero?" There are tears in her eyes. What the hell's going on?

"I'm sorry, Bobby. You'd better come in."

*

Author's note

These stories are gathered together in this the third collection to sit alongside *Openings and Endgame* and *Finder of Faces*. A fourth collection is being put together to come out in a few years' time. This final story won first prize in a competition and it has occurred to me that I should use it as the name for this little book.

I hope some of them will resonate, fill a quiet moment and set aside worries and thoughts that are causing anxiety, sadness and stress.

London, Dollis Hill Lane, spring and autumn 2022

*